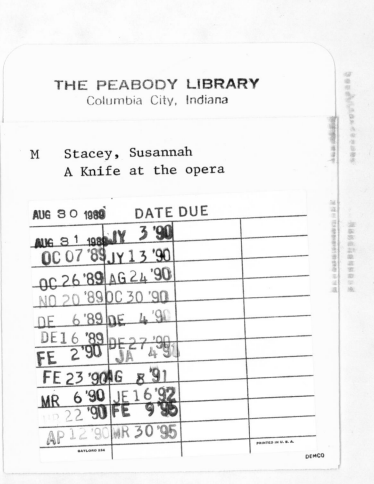

A Knife at the Opera

Susannah Stacey

SUMMIT BOOKS

NEW YORK   LONDON   TORONTO
SYDNEY   TOKYO

SUMMIT BOOKS
SIMON & SCHUSTER BUILDING
ROCKEFELLER CENTER
1230 AVENUE OF THE AMERICAS
NEW YORK, NEW YORK 10020

DISPLAY DESIGNED BY AMY BROWN
MANUFACTURED IN THE UNITED STATES OF AMERICA

1   3   5   7   9   10   8   6   4   2

LIBRARY OF CONGRESS CATALOGING IN PUBLICATION DATA

ISBN 0-671-65780-1 PBK.

A Knife at the Opera

CHAPTER
1

*The knife in his pocket was there still; he felt the smooth lines of it
as he walked along. It was so easy to buy, and he had wondered
why the girl he bought it from didn't know why he was buying it.
They had a way of knowing things like that—it was called mind-
reading.*

*He found he was keeping his eyes on the ground, noticing the
cracks in the pavement, the rubbish that blew in the gutter. The
cracks were interesting and you had to watch them, of course, in case
anything came out of them but he must remember he had to be looking
out for her. He must keep his eyes peeled. He thought a bit about
peeling eyes and decided it would be difficult but, once you had got
the hang of it, probably not much harder than peeling grapes.*

In the same town of Tunbridge Wells, at Hazeley, Grattan, the
estate agents, Michael Hazeley stared angrily out of the window, listening to the telephone. If the school secretary, at the
other end of the line (herself busily sorting letters, as she
replied in the pleasant soothing voice she kept particularly for
parents), could have seen the brilliant blue glare, she would
still not have dreamt of disturbing a teacher during class. Had
it been anyone with legitimate standing, such as a husband, he
would already have had the staffroom number. His peremptory
voice was lessening her patience.

'It's important. It's very important. Do you tell me there is
no way of getting hold of her? No, I can't leave my number.
Surely during school hours she is in the school?'

He listened, but cut in.

'Look: I'm not playing silly games. Damn it to hell, the school's not so enormous that you don't know where she is . . . Speak to you like what? How was I speaking to you? . . . Swearing? Who's swearing? . . . Just tell me, if it's not too much to ask, what time I *can* get hold of her?'

He listened; but at the explanation he smacked the receiver down and, after a moment of rigid fury, raised an arm and swept it with force across his desk, sending a cascade of blotter, in-tray, Christmas cards, files and pens to the floor. He was already putting his coat on when his secretary scuttled in.

'Is anything—oh, Mr Hazeley!'

'An accident,' he said. 'I'm late for my appointment.'

He brushed past her and left her staring at the mess on the floor, which was topped by an enragingly jolly Father Christmas.

In the Physics lab of the same school, Miss Wallace fiddled with her untidy hair, which no hairdresser had been allowed to make fashionable since, at twelve years old, she had looked in the mirror and liked what she saw. Her large dark eyes roved anxiously, trying to gather the class attention; looking, Beverly Braun decided, like a dog that wanted to pee and couldn't think how to cock its leg.

Four-L were studying the ripple tank. A less conscientious teacher than Miss Wallace would have left this particular group in ignorance of the properties of water waves, but she had set up the tank, as she always did, on four of the lab tables. These had originally been supplied with rubber feet, some of which had worn away or been peeled off by experiment-minded girls, leaving the desks unstable. She had had to find four with equal feet. Not for the first time, she regretted the solid, stained-pine benches of her own schooldays.

The display unit was a shallow plastic tray with an overhead light and a transparent floor. The designer had cleverly stipulated removable legs under each corner, which pushed into recesses and whose ball-socket, levelling feet provided an additional source of wave movement extraneous to the exercise.

'Stand *back*,' Miss Wallace called. 'Alison, Caroline, don't crowd so. You make it wobble.'

'I can't see at all.'

'Yes, of course. Let Perdita come to the front. No, let her, Emma.'

'I wasn't stopping her,' one Emma protested sweetly.

'Emma *Phillips*. Let Perdita come forward.'

Beverly Braun took Emma Phillips' collar and hauled her backwards, propelling Perdita to the front.

'Thank you, Beverly, but you need not—stand *back*, everybody. You must be sensible. Don't touch the desks.'

A surge from two in front jerked the water from the shallow tray. It slopped onto the desks and ran from there onto the girls' skirts and feet. An universal outcry was set up, from those who were wet and those who suffered their recoil. The sponge thoughtfully supplied with the apparatus came into play. Beverly then slapped it into the remaining water on the desks. Miss Wallace squirrelled it out of range and began the demonstration, in the partly justified hope that something actually happening would catch their interest and quieten them. She made one girl dip a ruler in, and instructed them to look at the shadows of ripples on the desk surfaces beneath.

'May I be excused please?' Perdita asked.

'You'll miss the experiment.'

'What rotten luck,' someone said.

'No, I can't wait.'

The rest laughed unkindly. Given permission, Perdita barged her way out. Having dried the table tops, Miss Wallace put a sheet of white paper under the tank to show the shadows more clearly. 'Now, you see the different ripples when I dip my finger.'

'How *poetic*,' said a flat voice. Laughter.

'Now, I hook this beam onto the rubber bands, and we can have a continuous ripple.' She picked up the control box. 'Stand back, everybody. Don't be so silly, pushing like that. You aren't the first-years. This is a serious demonstration.'

Someone said 'Serious moonlight', and someone began to sing a funeral march. As Miss Wallace switched the motor on, Alison spread her arms and leant back like a crowd-control policeman. It was effective, but Mairi Leggatt, backing, tripped over the electric cable and pulled the plug from the socket. The motor went dead.

They cheered.

'Put it back, Mairi.' Miss Wallace managed bright patience.

'Shouldn't she switch off first?'

'Mairi's *always* switched off,' a tired voice said.

'Yes, well, put the switch off, Mairi.'

Mairi, a slender girl with a cloud of hair, crouched by the wall and, after a moment, said plaintively, 'It won't go in.'

Some ribald murmur and a gust of giggles; Emma Jones bent down and rammed the plug in and switched on. The motor started, causing little shrieks of surprise. The overhead light flung shadows of the waves, and there came momentary quiet as the class looked at these.

'Pretty.'

'Just like the sand under the sea.'

'More like the baths with the wave machine, only that's bigger and better than this.'

To counter this denigration, Miss Wallace put the curved barrier into the tray, altering the pattern. They watched that for three seconds.

'I don't see what it's in aid of,' Beverly Braun remarked. She was a tall girl, large, with dead-black hair and, in defiance of school rules, heavily made-up eyes. 'I mean most of Physics is what you'd expect, right? Common sense. Waves make patterns, okay, and the patterns alter when you put things in the way. What's the big deal?'

'But it's how they alter that is so important. Water *and* air waves and sound ... ' she was going into an explanation of what to her was profoundly interesting when a noise of cascading water and violent screams drowned her out. The stopper had somehow come loose in the tray.

An unlikely amount of water flooded the tables. Girls scrambled out of the way knocking over the stools. In an interesting manifestation of physical law and of some fault in the flooring, the water ran into a shallow puddle near the door. Someone, trying to climb upon a stool, upset the waste-bin into this. The bell rang.

As Four-L gathered up their belongings Miss Wallace got

her back to the door. She announced, in a high voice not devoid of panic, 'No one is leaving this room until the mess is all cleared up.'

They surged towards her, those behind pushing cheerfully, thrusting the front of the crowd against Miss Wallace. Caroline fended herself off with a hand to the door. Under all their feet, the torn paper pashed and was pulped.

'Come on, Wally.' Someone safely at the back used the nickname. 'We'll be late for lunch.'

'We didn't make this mess.'

'—Was an accident.'

'Not our fault. And there's Opera dress-rehearsal.'

'No one leaves this room until it's cleared up, so get the cloths from the sink-cupboard.'

A vague move to do this was halted by an unseen gesture.

'No one leaves!'

A voice at the back imitated with vicious accuracy, 'No one!' There was a general happy laugh. Miss Wallace saw nothing but smiles in the scrum; they were, they implied, all joking. Only some eyes kept a watchful curiosity. Caroline reached for the door handle, turned it and began to pull the door open.

'Let us go, Miss Wallace. We'll be late.'

'Come on, Wally, be a nice kind person.'

'We'll come and clear up after lunch. Honest!'

'Yes, we'll clear up after.'

The door jerked against her back, the girls crushed forwards. They were too close. Emma Jones lost her footing and her head hit Miss Wallace's shoulder.

'Pack it in, you at the back, we're getting squashed.'

'Everybody out!'

Then a burst of song: 'Why are we wai-ting?'

They all took it up, stamping on the floor, with a ripple effect from those in the water. A wooden thunder of knocking sounded from outside and the door opened forcefully, sending Miss Wallace into the throng and hitting Caroline's knuckles. As Four-L, who had been hushed for a second, saw who it was coming in, they shrieked a welcome. 'Miss Fairlie, Miss Fairlie!' and a whistle from someone, a few notes from the entrance of the Sugar Plum fairy from *Nutcracker*. She smiled round, dimples showing in a small, pointed face; she had an abundance of dark hair curling to her shoulders, and blue eyes surrounded surprisingly by thick dark lashes.

'What a noise. What on earth were you doing? No, I can't hear you! Alison, you tell me.'

'We were trying to go to lunch and Miss Wallace said we must clear up first, but we didn't make this mess, it was an accident.'

Miss Fairlie discovered Miss Wallace behind the door. 'Oh,' she said, 'I didn't think you could be here, with all this noise.' She turned to the girls once more. 'Well, then, if it was an accident, you're not responsible for it, are you?'

Chorus: 'No, Miss Fairlie.'

'Then don't keep the dinner ladies waiting. See you all at rehearsal!' She stepped aside and they streamed through the door between the two women, splashing water into the corridor. Several said, 'Thank you, Miss Fairlie,' as they went.

Claire Fairlie turned to go. Smiling at Miss Wallace, she said, 'Why don't you tell Harry Birch to clear this up? It's his job, you know. Tell Harry Birch I said he was to clear this up.'

Judy Fazackerly, of Two-F, bounced into the doorway of Harry Birch's den. She liked running errands, even for the Wally and even to Birch. He put down the chair he was mending and came to the door. She backed slightly.

'What can I do for you, then, darling?'

His jersey had holes in over the bulge of his stomach, his zip was a bit undone. He smiled: his two top chins were stubbly, the chin that should have been his neck was smooth. There were hairs in his nose.

'Miss Wallace says Miss Fairlie says will you go and clean up the Physics lab before two o'clock please.'

'Miss Wallace says—?'

'She says Miss Fairlie says—'

'Can't make head nor tail of that, can I? Who sent you?'

'Miss Wallace.' Judy grabbed her tights through her skirt and hitched, wriggling. Birch's smile widened.

'Miss Wallace? No hurry then.'

'She says Miss Fairlie says.'

'All right, all right. It'll get done. Have a toffee?' He was reaching for the tin, but Judy shook her head.

'Spoil my lunch,' she said, and turned and ran. She could feel his eyes on her legs all the way, running up like a ladder.

'That's funny.'

'What?' More of Four-G looked out of the windows.

'Didn't you see?' Prudence Grant asked.

'Would I be asking if I had?' Kat Hazeley demanded.

'Really weird, it was. Our noble Deputy Head unlocking her car, and then she just scrunched down behind it. Just like she didn't want to be seen.'

'Mrs Lambert? Didn't want to be seen by who?'

'She's heavily in debt and it's the bailiff.' Last lesson had been Social History.

'She saw Miss Mallett at her window pulling the pin out of a grenade.' The Headmistress' window also overlooked the front of the school.

'She's really a Russian agent. In the Death Squad.'

'You imagined it, poor demented Prue.'

Charlotte Bone said, 'I saw too.'

'Are you sure that if you weren't Prue's best friend you would have seen it?' Kat asked, her head on one side.

'No. I saw.'

'The Lamb crouched behind her car?'

'Uh-huh.'

'What did she do then? Her car's gone.'

Prue said, 'She sort of slid into the driving seat and drove off. All very James Bond.'

'But who was there to be hiding from?'

Prue stood her hair further on end with both hands and shrugged. 'Street full of people. She was parked just outside the gates.'

'She'd dropped something and bent to pick it up, you clot.'

'I tell you she was all secretive.'

Charlotte, appealed to, shrank with furtive speed down beside the radiator, then sideways into a chair. Prue said that was it exactly. 'Weird, it was.'

She and Charlotte were both relatively new girls, coming

last Summer from the same school. Charlotte Bone, who was lame and could not speak clearly, had taken a bit of getting used to; Prue, the joker, almost too much at home too soon, was protective of her. Both were now popular, Prue for subversive humour, Charlotte for good nature and for her dauntless struggle with the demons of speech and locomotion. Indeed, she spoke far more clearly these days, towards the end of her second term at Haddon House.

Charlotte had inadvertently caused a revelation of humanity in Sir Herbert Derwent, the visiting music master; his prestige as a composer made his school post seem almost condescension and he maintained an aloofness considered snooty, but he had given Charlotte the routine voice test and, discovering purity of tone and a good ear, told her to leave out any consonants she couldn't yet sing and get on with the music. Her voice was, in fact, out of the ordinary, and she could sing what she could not say. The form were proud of her. She was surprised by this, and did not in the least mind being called Charred Bone, Charcoal, or Chariot; though Skeleton, or Skelly, were Prue Grant's prerogative. Anyone was allowed to call Prudence 'Grue'.

Beverly Braun, zipping her blazer's inner pocket shut on the cardboard tube of tablets, stood foursquare, all but fivesquare, looking at Mairi Leggatt. The cloakroom lay empty around the three of them. Mairi, whooping laughter, dashed along the aisle between lockers, fetched up against the end wall and stood there banging her head on a locker door.

'She's had too much,' said the girl at Beverly's side.

'She hasn't, then. You've had that much before now.'

'But what'll she do in rehearsal?'

Beverly, still watching under the black strands of her hair, tucked her mouth into what might be a smile. 'What d'you think?'

'She'll make a hash of Mrs Trapse.'

'Going to fuck up the Sugar Plum's rehearsal,' Beverly agreed. 'Shame, isn't it?'

'But what about tonight and the Opera? Will Fairlie let you sing it?'

Beverly shrugged.

'Suppose someone finds her now?'

'Who would?'

'Harry Birch.'

They both laughed shortly. '*He'll* know what to do.'

Mairi had subsided to the floor and was singing 'Sailing' in a maudlin croak. Beverly pushed her crony ahead of her out of the door, and they went upstairs.

In Parloe Road, a street of genteel small houses, semi-detached, eighteen eighties, with barge-boarded eaves and fake concrete keystones to the architraves, two men stood on a tiled front-garden path. The Colonel wore a small moustache, like a frosty rime surviving the habitual red heat of his face.

'Of course it's lowering the neighbourhood.'

The Colonel's voice had the carrying power and derogatory tone of his class. He and his departing guest eyed the offence. His own miniature front garden was filled with roses behind a neat privet hedge. The neighbours' held trampled earth, children's toys, a roll of wire netting, a plastic bowl, about forty discarded ring-pulls and was dominated by a large motor-bike.

'When the Boldings left, we certainly didn't expect to be landed with this sort of thing. Estate agents ought to consider the tone of a neighbourhood. Property values will plummet once people like this move in.'

'Very unpleasant.'

'Noisy. Punk children with their loud music. Should be another word for it, not music at all; and their sort never speak. Always shout.'

'Pretty unfortunate.'

'You'd think they would feel sufficiently out of place. You'd think they'd look around, see how people here behaved, adapt themselves. Not a bit of it. Bring their damned slum ways with them. They haven't the intelligence. Nothing but cheek. They have any amount of that.'

A motor-bike cruised down the street, stopping outside the despised neighbours' house and decanting its pillion passenger in tooled high-heeled boots, tight leather pants and dayglo green anorak.

'Ta-ra then.' Taking off its helmet, the passenger revealed

itself as a girl, shaking heavy gleaming blonde hair into place. The bike roared off down the street as she took the few paces up her garden, said 'Hallo' to the Colonel in an amused voice, let herself in and yelled, 'Mum! I'm back!' as she shut the door.

'You hear that. And "Hallo". Damned familiar. D'you know what they do when their dustbin's full up? They dump their damned rubbish in our bin.'

'Inconvenient.'

'Inconvenient! Bottles and junk-food packets. No room for the rest of our own stuff, and an electricity bill with their name on in the midst of it all, so that it was plain where it came from. I took the whole lot and dumped it beside their bin in the alley—I showed them that sort of cheek just wasn't on. Put the lot back where it belonged.'

'What happened?'

'Dustmen left it, of course; they won't take loose stuff. So the Jenkinses knew what I'd done, all right. D'you know what then? Woman came round and told my wife it was unneighbourly.'

'No, really?'

'Dump their damn stuff in our bin and then when we object they call it "unneighbourly". M'wife said to her that in this sort of neighbourhood people have very different ideas, and she shut the door on her.'

A radio had started in the next house. A shouted exchange, evidently between downstairs and up, battled with its noise.

'Intolerable,' the Colonel said. He added, 'Worst of it is, we can't move. House prices, y'know.'

'Surely you'd get quite a bit for this one?'

'With that crew next door?'

'They bought a house here. Their friends might.'

'Good God! More of them?'

'You wouldn't be here to suffer from it if you'd moved away.'

'M'm. True. Pity of it is, we liked the place. Happy here.' He champed his lip. 'Really damnable.'

The Games teacher had a way of opening the staffroom door that made everyone inside feel guilty, however innocent their occupation. Most of them were eating lunch, Miss Wallace tidy at the ink-stained table, unpacking her lunch-box with meticulous slowness that gave a dreadful idea of how long it took to prepare and pack it at home. She had been crying, and her nose shone defiantly through the powder she had patched onto it. Mrs Garland, who taught Domestic Science, after watching these proceedings for a moment, rolled her eyes and undid a Cornish pasty from foil. With an air of one who refrains from saying 'snap!' so did Miss Fairlie; Mrs Garland sourly reflected that while she could herself legitimately take her demonstration item of food for lunch, Miss Fairlie had only to flatter one of her dedicated band to con them out of theirs. She wondered which of the third year was not taking their Cornish pasty home.

'Five pounds gone this time,' said the Games teacher, closing the door. 'Mary Parkin. *From* her locker. *Which* she says she locked.' Having machine-gunned them with this information, she looked round triumphantly. Mrs Garland cupped a hand snaring an escaped piece of potato, and shrugged. Miss Wallace, her back so carefully to everyone, put a small plastic salt-shaker on the table and unfolded a paper napkin. Claire Fairlie laughed.

'Tell Baa-Lamb. It'll be the last straw after Mally's sermon on stealing in Assembly. She'll get her knickers in such a twist she won't walk straight for a week.'

At that moment Baa-Lamb herself opened the door and provoked fresh laughter in the beautiful Miss Fairlie. 'You look terrible. Been mugged for your library tickets, or did you bump into Bev Braun running downstairs?'

Miss Wallace, interested to learn that someone might look worse than she did, risked a quick look round her shoulder. Mrs Lambert did look very pale, quite as though she had seen a ghost. She received the news of the theft with abstraction, and Miss Wallace thought—picking up her plastic knife to cut her lettuce sandwich in half—if you really did see a ghost it would, of course, tend to make everything else less important. *Turning* some people into ghosts round here might settle matters even better.

'*May* I get past you girls?'

'Sorry, Mr Sharpe.' His bitter presence parted them like a sword. Julia Craven, not an imaginative girl, thought he smelt of anger. At the top of the stairs he paused, hesitated, and looked down at them.

'Have you seen Miss Fairlie?'

They hadn't, though one of them thought she was out shopping, and another believed she was coaching some Opera people in her lunch-hour. Mr Sharpe listened, frowning, and his eyes watched something else in his mind. He interrupted another suggestion that Miss Fairlie might be in the library.

'Never mind. It doesn't matter.'

As he turned away he thought he heard them giggling but, as she had said herself, schoolgirls *always* giggle.

They had said she would be here and they were never wrong. Sometimes, though, he didn't listen carefully enough—there was so much going on that you had to watch, so perhaps they hadn't said 'today'. He would find her tomorrow. That was it. Tomorrow was another day. Barbara used to say that and it was very comforting really. After all, the knife would wait. All over the world knives were waiting.

He had forgotten to look at the cracks in the pavement and now he stumbled. There was a blazer lying there, crumpled and dirty, probably fallen off the wall. He picked it up and looked round. Only a milk float rattling down the street, and a small dog watering a lamp-post. He took out the knife and slit the blazer over the heart, in a neat cross. The cloth was difficult to cut, but the knife was very sharp and he did not lack persistence or strength.

When it was done, he hung the blazer on one of the spikes of the railing and put his knife back in his pocket. It had needed practice.

CHAPTER
2

Prue rapped on her brother's door. 'Open up. Police.'

'What you want?' he shouted, muting the rock blare slightly.

'Your shirts. For the opera. You said you'd lend.'

He unlocked the door. 'Root them out for yourself; but show me; I mightn't want to part.' Gesturing at the drawers, he returned to the bed and dropped down among cassettes and magazines.

Prue burrowed her way through the drawers' chaos, tossing a shirt or two onto the floor behind her, inspecting others.

'You can't have that one.'

'Oh look, I only want it because it's messy. You can't wear it until it's washed anyway. Dead suitable for a highwayman.'

'Oh well, what's it matter, take the lot.'

Prue bundled her choice together and grinned at Martin. They were much alike, dark, with long mouths rather full of teeth, and upright hairdos, but her face was alive.

'You feeling rotten again?'

'Buzz off, kid.'

'Okay *okay*, only asked. Will you be there tonight?'

'Will it be any good, or just girls'-school stuff?'

'We had a *filthy* dress-rehearsal, so it should be good. Sugar Plum Fairlie went spare. The highwaymen in school shirts looked just stupid, "Peachum" kept crying, and Mairi Leggatt went barmy, she just fell about all over the stage. Darling Claire sent her home—took her home, I think—and she's going to sing Mrs Trapse herself.'

'Who is? Fairlie?'

'Yes, dumbo, Fairlie, your English coach.'

'Who's Mrs Trapse?'

'A madam.'

He lay back. 'I'll probably come,' he said.

Charlotte Bone hovered by the table where her father was typing. He made a mistake, stopped, reached for the paper-paint and said, 'Get it off your chest.'

'Well, a) you will come, won't you? and b) can I borrow the pewter mug, the big one?'

'Dad's tankard? I don't want it dented and scratched. I've a strong memory of backstage scrums from my own schooldays.'

'I'll hold it all the time, myself.'

'All right. But don't dump it and forget it when the show's over.'

'Thanks.' She kissed his head, the same pale gold as her own but less bright, threaded with grey. 'And—'

His hands over the keys, he said, 'If I don't finish this I can't come anyway.'

'Fibs. Daddy, could you, *could* you, just take the phone off the hook? You're not on duty.'

'I can't, Cha. You know I can't.'

'No, I suppose . . .' she sighed. 'Remember I'm the highway-man on the end at the left—no, the right from your side. All made up villainous so you won't re-cog-nise.'

'My instinct will be to arrest you all on the spot.'

'Once you get there you will be really off duty,' she said. 'They can't bother you there.'

Bone took his seat in the school Hall, in the pleasant, expectant hum of an audience. Though he was by this time familiar with quite a few of the parents, none he knew was sitting nearby, and he liked the solitude. Ahead of him the Hall platform had fitup curtains, shifting sometimes to a draught or movement behind them. A small orchestra made tentative sounds. He read his programme, finding Charlotte at the foot among 'Highway-men' and oddly pleased to read her name. There was Grue's name too, among 'Ladies of the Town'. She had said, 'I'm just a supernumerary trull.'

Here came Miss Dunne, Cha's English teacher, young enough to look like one of the girls out of uniform, her thick, tawny hair flying; hurrying by with an armful of props, evading a parent, vanishing backstage.

Ursula Dunne made her way among chorus and bit-part singers to the soloists' dressing-room. When the school was built during the late nineteenth century, theatre had not been considered as a legitimate pastime, so backstage arrangements were far from ideal. To reach the other side of the stage one had to go round by the playground, and at the moment a constant two-way flow was doing so. Claire Fairlie, already in a long skirt and low-cut blouse, was helping 'Mrs Peachum' to look overblown. She was not made up herself yet, and Ursula had a fleeting uncharitable thought that perhaps we were to get a young and blooming Mrs Trapse (in defiance of the lyric about her fled youth); 'Macheath', Sarah Crouch, tried on his tricorne before the glass with a debonair flourish.

'Your pistols, Macheath,' Ursula said.

'Stap me vitals, ma'am, I thought I'd still have to mime them.' He stuck the wooden objects into his belt. Miss Dunne delivered a poison bottle to Lucy Lockit, money to Peachum, handkerchiefs to Filch, and checked on the stage props, then on the costumes. To her surprise, everything lacking that morning and afternoon had been brought; the girls having suddenly realised that 'some time' for which they had to provide them, and which had comfortably always been in the future, was now. One highwayman was still short of a waistcoat—'Mother's bringing it, but I could go on without it—' her figure was such as to render a waistcoat imperative. She wanted to go out to the curtains to wait for it, despite all commands to stay put. Miss Dunne went out instead. At the door from backstage into the Hall, Tabi St John stood resisting with prefectly firmness the pleas of various beggars to be allowed out to see if their parents were there. Tabitha shooed them aside to let Miss Dunne out.

In the wings, Mr Sharpe waited. He had volunteered for the difficult task of keeping order and quiet there, and on this side of the stage order and quiet were sure to obtain. She did not exactly like Mr Sharpe, but admired his energetic discipline.

In the odd light here behind the curtains, his tight face looked to be in pain rather than merely disagreeable.

When the overture struck up, and the Hall lights were darkened, Bone felt an unexpected excitement. It was a long time since he had been at the theatre; too long. He didn't even get to see a film much these days. It might be he was in danger of turning reclusive. After Petra's death he'd not wanted to go about; Charlotte needed company; they had become self-sufficient. He had been surprised by the deadness of his own feelings.

The audience, quietened by the darkness and by the music, began to talk again when they found that the curtains did not rise. Surely in the old days, in his boyhood, people did not do that? They listened to overtures, in anticipation. Now, when nothing was before their eyes, they talked. But the curtains parted; the Beggar emerged, to announce his authorship of the opera. Rags and dirt so convinced that the girl's voice came as a surprise.

Peachum had made an effort at a villainous voice, revelling in double-dealing with quite professional aplomb. Once you got used to girls' voices—this one and Macheath had strong contraltos—you could appreciate that it was well done; a matter of accepting an idiom.

Backstage, Lucy Lockit, panicking because her pregnancy had slipped, was rescued by a highwayman: Charlotte Bone found a kilt pin among the mess at the bottom of the make-up box, and secured the cushion to the webbing braces. Miss Dunne watched with approval, but was at this moment called away by Tabitha to quieten the highwaymen who were already in the wings.

As she pulled the excited group apart and laid her finger on her lips before each one, Mr Sharpe appeared above them on the stage before the side curtain and came down the steps. He was breathing so deeply that it was noticeable, and his neat round face was so pinched that it looked savage. There was silence, the girls fell still. Under that basilisk glare no one moved.

The little orchestra sounded really rather good, she thought. The piano, under the hands of Sachiko Fujiwara, one of the school's most gifted pupils, was the mainstay, doing much of the complicated stuff that the clarinet, two violins and guitar were not up to.

Someone pulled her sleeve. Prue Grant, garishly bedizened, her blouse pulled so low that only just was it decent, drew her back into the dressing-rooms.

'Is Miss Fairlie round here? She's on any moment.'

Miss Dunne managed not to ask a silly question, 'Isn't she round your side?' and said no, she hadn't seen her; with a word to Tabitha she hurried out of the door at the back, across to the twin entrance the other side, and found a hustle of harlots in the passage spilling from their dressing-room. The cold from the playground, and Ursula, sent them back into the warmth, all bosoms and petticoats, too much make-up and blacked-out teeth. Ursula investigated the prompt-side wings. There was Samantha Macgregor with the prompt book, Anne Higgins as Filch, Fazileh the prefect. On the edge of the stage was a pile of dumped properties and clothes. She mouthed to Fazileh, 'Where's Mrs Lambert?'

'Looking in the staff loo.'

Ursula peeked through the side curtains that hid the wings from the Hall. No sign. She tried the Domestic Science room door where Claire was supposed to be making up. Locked. She rapped softly.

'We did that,' muttered Prue, 'and I looked in from outside. She's not there. Her mirror's there and the make-up box.'

'Mairi's not here, is she?'

'No.'

They stood in the dark corridor a moment. Fazileh opened the door from the wings and said 'Miss Fairlie's scene's starting.'

'Oh God,' Prue moaned.

'We should have stopped them. Had an interval while we search. We can't now. Or should we?' Ursula envisaged going on stage to do so and her nerve failed. 'We'll have to stop them.'

She turned towards the stage. A solid figure carrying a large black hat stood in her way.

'I can sing it,' said Beverly Braun, and waved the hat. 'I was supposed to do it when we started last term.'

Too glad to ask any questions, Ursula propelled her towards the stage—not that she had to. Beverly paused in the wings to do only one thing—dab powder messily on the sides of her dense black hair and put the hat on. Anne Higgins playing the servant was at this moment announcing, though she glanced back anxiously, 'Mrs Trapse is below.' She was not sure if she should do this or what would happen, but dared not miss her cue. No Miss Fairlie arrived from nowhere. Beverly poised herself on the steps and, as Anne Higgins passed her, she hoisted her skirts and pranced sturdily on stage.

Bone was aware that the actors on stage were startled. The girl in the black hat was not Miss Fairlie, as the announcement had said. It was the Molly Brazen of the previous scene, grey-haired to be sure and, as she moved, indefinably middle-aged. This was no Molly Brazen. She had a raucous gin voice, full of innuendo, with none of Molly's surface of gentility, and as she launched into song it was pure music-hall: *In the days of my youth I could bill like a dove*—she gave the audience a swift sidelong glance and made an unspeakable undulation with her whole stout body. Bone started to grin.

In the wings Ursula stood, mouth ajar. Beverly had taken the stage as her own. What parents might think of this performance would come out later, but it was a masterpiece. Lockit had been thrown by the advent of Beverly and was coping but no more. Peachum, inspired, answered deep to deep. *Fal-la-la-la-la*, they rollicked arm in arm, bumped hips, flirted, *fa la-la-la la-la*; their voices suggested an ancient and long-lived affaire; how did girls know these things?

Behind Ursula craned a gaggle of stunned trollops watching, delighted. When Mrs Trapse tossed her skirts up at Peachum and he responded with a leer they clapped hands to mouths and looked to see how Ursula was taking it.

As applause burst from the audience, Ursula drove the girls out of the wings and into their dressing-room, to which she admitted Beverly flapping powder from her hair and panting, to be embraced like a football hero. She let herself out and, holding the door in the cool darkness of the passage, wondered where Claire Fairlie was.

Bone thought that the rest of the opera might be something

anti-climactic after that joyous little riot; but John Gay was no
fool. He had devised a change of tone, where Macheath,
recaptured, is doomed to die. The stage filled with a watchful
crowd. Lucy and Polly began the minor-key trio with Macheath
in their despair:

> *Would I might be hang'd—and I would so too—*
> *Would I might be hang'd, my dear, with you,*

He was so caught in the tragic mood of this song, with the
premonitory insistent sound of the bell, that its interruption
surprised him. A loud indignant voice broke in:

'But you would not have Macheath hanged?'

The Beggar pushed forward and insisted that indeed he
would. The moral was a necessity. Against this the whole cast
protested. The small child playing Filch now jumped up and
down and shrilled 'A reprieve, a reprieve!'

They took up the cry, overwhelmed the moral Beggar, and the
whole company whirled into a dance, a dance that overflowed
the stage and frisked down the aisles, circling and spinning
with the tune, Macheath's 'My heart was so free.' On stage
Mrs Trapse and Peachum, Lockit and Mrs Peachum, Macheath
and his wives, hopped and spun, circled, armed, kicked up
their heels, until the curtains closed on them.

They had all to take their bows and their curtsies. Applause
crashed round their ears. Bone's hands became hot from clapping. Even with the Hall lights on, parents and guests seemed
to think there must still be curtain calls; but at last the noise
died. People began to go. Parents of the performers still waited.
Martin Grant, at the back, sat moodily staring at his feet propped on the seat in front of him. The Grants themselves were
not visible. Bone wondered if the Leggatts were here, for he
supposed that Mairi Leggatt, recovered, must be the girl who
had played Mrs Trapse.

Some of the cast were going home as they were, others preferred to change. Charlotte must be changing. He waited. A girl ran
headlong among the groups in the far aisle. Miss Mallett, the
Head, trod back in the opposite direction, the girl at her heels; a
tall woman with grey hair in a soigné French pleat, wearing a
long sleeveless coat in olive and ochre tapestry that

looked mediaeval. She went through the curtains beside the stage.

Reappearing, she surveyed the audience for a moment, saw Bone, and crossed in front of the stage. He saw that she was making for him and rose to meet her, hurrying. His first premonition was for Charlotte.

She spoke in a low voice. 'Would you please come, Super-intendent? Something has happened to Miss Fairlie.'

The groups they passed stopped talk and turned. It was obvious from Miss Mallett's silence and her not stopping for social words that something serious had occurred, perhaps to this parent's daughter. The few who knew him broke into speculation: a police matter? Bone might indeed have worn the mask of his name as he followed Miss Mallett backstage.

CHAPTER

Miss Mallett led the way through the curtains, past the side of the stage still littered with clothes and props and a powder-box, a stool and an Anglepoise lamp, through the doors into the backstage. Straight ahead, double doors, half glassed, gave onto the playground. On the left, sobbing came from a room whose bright lights showed round the door. Mrs Lambert stood like a statue outside the door opposite. She had put a school sweater over her dress and her arms were crossed, hands gripping her shoulders. As Bone came near he could see she was rigid, so tense that she trembled.

Miss Mallett reached up and undid a bolt at the top of the door. She led Bone inside.

It was the D.S. room, not unlike the kitchen of a small hotel, the walls lined with cookers, sinks and work units. In the centre, work tables, with stools upended on them, faced the work and demonstration bench along the wall behind the door.

Behind the bench, arched over a stool so that her face was upside down, Miss Fairlie lay. Her brown hair cascaded to the floor. Blood had splashed the foot of the blackboard and run down the wall. Her mouth and eyes were open.

'Has anything been moved or touched?'

'Mr Sharpe was in here, holding her.'

'Where is he?'

'Mrs Tudor has taken him to sick-bay. He was—distraught. He was, you see, particularly attached to Miss Fairlie.'

Bone noted the fact of the attachment. From Miss Mallett's demeanour he also noted that Mr Sharpe—he taught German, didn't he?—was not considered by those who knew him to be a likely murderer. That Cha was terrified of German tests did not qualify the man as a homicide. Neither did these considerations disqualify him. Bone's priority must be to see Sharpe. Experience had taught him that the person found with the body is not necessarily the maker of the corpse. Meanwhile there was routine.

Bone had not so far become inured to this moment, of facing a human being dead. He had not seen so very many. He approached, bent down from a yard away for a closer look. Blood smelt strongly. It always brought back the same picture, the farmhouse kitchen of his school holidays, his aunt cleaning the game shot by her husband and Bone's father. The innocent birds lay with blood at their nostrils.

Under the body a thing like a crouched cat resolved itself as a red wig on the floor. Without gloves and proper slippers he would not go closer, although enough evidence had clearly been destroyed already. He paused suddenly to say to Miss Mallett, 'Have the police been called?' He saw from her hesitation that they had not. He was the police. He said, 'I'll do it now.'

He locked the door and took the key. 'Can those girls be moved further away? Are their parents here?'

'Of some of them. I thought they should stay until you had seen them, perhaps they might ... They can go to the other dressing-rooms on the opposite side.'

'Yes, please. Any whose parents aren't here I may not talk to without permission.'

'Mrs Lambert, please tell Miss Dunne to take them round to Room Seven. Would you like to use the telephone in my office?' At the doors she paused before entering the Hall and said, 'And Barbara, would you see if cups of tea could be organised? I am sure we are going to need some.'

'Yes, Miss Mallett.'

Bone recognised the masterly way in which a perturbed woman was got away from the girls and given something to do.

'Who has keys to that room?' he asked as they hurried through the Hall.

'Mrs Garland, the D.S. teacher, and there's a set in the secretary's office.'

A woman said, 'Will Tanya be long now?' from the chairs as they passed. Miss Mallett said, 'I hope not.'

Miss Mallett's room was carpeted, curtained, comfortable, and hot. The electric fire was on in the fireplace. There were high-backed easy chairs covered in tapestry, and bookcases, and a large desk. Miss Mallett put on the desk light and went out.

He telephoned headquarters and it was agreed that he should take the case as he was there. He asked for the whole shooting-match to be sent round. It was Monday night; they would be pleased. He sighed. He needn't ring Charlotte to say he'd be late. He must see her, see if she was all right.

Miss Mallett was keeping parents in conversation in the entrance hall. He caught her eye and she came calmly, unhurriedly over. He backed into her room.

'When the squad comes I'll take them round the side and in at the back,' he said. 'About interviewing the girls: we can do that, with their parents' permission, in your presence, or in a parent's presence if a parent is here. I don't suppose any of them has seen or knows anything, but if their parents aren't here, could they be phoned for permission?'

Miss Mallett said, 'Miss Cantrell, the secretary, is still here. She will do that as soon as we find who is still here with no parents. So far no one has been told. Shall I do that?'

'I think you must. Unless you wish me to?'

A blue radiance lit the entrance hall. Bone said, 'No, my crew is here.'

Miss Mallett called to the waiting group in the entrance lobby, 'Will you come into Hall, please?' and Bone went out down the steps, remembering Charlotte saying, 'Once you get there you'll be really off duty. They can't bother you there.'

He left one P.C., a young man he didn't know well, to direct reinforcements round to the back, and took the uniform sergeant and the photographer who had also arrived round with him. They had hardly reached the scene of the crime when

Detective-Inspector Steve Locker arrived. He had buttoned his shirt askew and looked rumpled, his dark hair on end.

'Caught me on my way to bed,' he said. Bone swung a wrist to check the time, and Steve said, 'Kid's teething, not a wink last night, trying for an early kip.'

'Here's your field, Steve. Deceased is Claire Fairlie, teacher at the school. The body's been disturbed at least once; I'll be sorting out that one shortly but I'd like to see what girls are still here and how Charlotte is.'

'Right oh.'

Bone looked briefly into the empty dressing-room on that side, where lights burned down on pushed-aside desks, a few belongings, a black hat. He crossed the curtained stage, so late a scene of triumph, and came to the corresponding rooms on the other side. He could hear parental voices desultorily in the Hall, muted, shocked.

Charlotte, ready dressed although in trousers, boots and sweater she looked not so different from the highwayman, was no longer grime-faced. She sat with her feet stretched before her, nursing his father's pewter tankard between her knees. She was slumped a little, and the face she raised reminded him of the way she had been after the accident, after her return from hospital, for long weeks, drawn and shocked. He put out an arm and she got up and came to him. He kissed her eyebrow and asked in a private murmur, 'All right, chick?' His arm closed on her thinness. The waiting girls, and Miss Dunne watched the police evince humanity with tired interest.

'Yes. Okay,' she said.

He looked round at the others. 'We'll be as quick as we can and let you go home. Hallo, Prue.'

Prue said, 'It was me that went in there. It would be, wouldn't it?' Her bony face, too, looked peaked and the effort at brightness showed.

'Your nose goes everywhere,' Cha said. She was trying to smile. He could not remember if she had ever said she liked Miss Fairlie or how well she knew her. Miss Dunne was her English teacher.

'I'd better talk to you, Prue. Your mother here?'

'No one's here. Martin was.'

The winter dark beyond the windows suddenly flickered blue-white from photo-flash in the D.S. A girl gasped.

'As good as TV,' Bone said, cooling it. 'Police everywhere.'

'Different when it's real,' someone said.

'I'm sorry. Can I just ask all of you here if you saw anything unusual around backstage tonight? Or noticed anything odd. Apart from the absence of Miss Fairlie.'

They looked at each other. Heads shook.

'We thought,' said a maternal-looking senior with a prefect's badge on her purple and green tie, 'that it went so well.' Her voice wavered. There was a silence. Torches swung in the playground.

'It was a magnificent performance,' Bone said. 'That really happened and can't be taken away.' But subsequent happenings did alter the way things were perceived, and therefore, subtly, alter the things themselves.

'She was the producer,' said a blonde girl in a too-tight sweater.

'Then everyone did her proud,' Bone said. There was a gruff 'Sir,' behind him and he turned to see Sergeant Gurr. With a quick reassurance to Charlotte, Bone joined him in the corridor. Gurr shut the door on the girls and said, 'Found the weapon, sir.'

A drawer in the D.S. room had been pulled out by the searchers. Among knives, some plastic-sheathed, and palette knives, a smeared blade lay slewed across the rest.

'We've got pictures,' the photographer said.

'Prints?' Bone stood back for the man who had been busy on the handle and rim of the drawer. After a moment or two the man shrugged.

'Wiped pretty thoroughly, like this drawer.'

Bone regarded the knife lying, innocent of its misuse, the plain kitchen blade perhaps six inches long, quite broad, the wood handle studded with two brass pins.

'Check with the D.S. teacher—Miss—Mrs Garland?—that it belongs here. It's like the others. The girls on the other side, Steve—' They had a word or two about getting accounts of the evening from those who had been on this side. Bone wanted to send Charlotte home. He couldn't question Prue without parental leave which perhaps Miss Cantrell had succeeded in getting by now; if not, he would send Charlotte to Prue's; Martin Grant could take them. Going through the Hall, however, he saw no Martin.

His request to see Mr Sharpe was answered by the eruption, ahead of the escorting constable, of a small dark man whose jacket fronts, waistcoat and tie were smeared with blood.

'What's happening? Who is in charge?'

Miss Mallett had offered her room for Bone to work in, and she was about to depart into her secretary's office next door. She said, 'Detective-Superintendent Bone,' with slightly repressive emphasis, indicating him with a simple dramatic waft of the hand, and went out.

'I'm not going to be shut up like a lunatic in the sickroom with a warder keeping an eye on me. I didn't kill her—did you think I had? Do you think I would? Claire—I had asked her to marry me.'

Bone did not point out that this was no reason why he had not killed her. He said, 'Won't you sit down, Mr Sharpe?'

'I will not sit down!' His agitation was pathetic because it was ludicrous. His hands made pawing movements. 'What's being done? Have you taken her away?'

'We're starting an enquiry, Mr Sharpe.'

'Well, then,' said Mr Sharpe. He seemed to be in no doubt about who was conducting the interview. 'What is being done?'

'Did you know where she was, Mr Sharpe? During the opera?'

'She was using the room as a dressing-room, I understood, although she was not there when first I looked for her. Then she refused to talk to me. Evading, always evading me, as if I had no reason for concern or nothing to do with her at all. Perfectly self-possessed. Teasing, yes. Always ready to tease but never serious. She won't—*would not*,' he corrected himself with a desolate rise in tone, 'discuss the situation. She would not take me seriously.' His face expressed how incredible he felt this to be. He was perhaps Bone's age, or a little older, perhaps forty, from touches of grey at the temples. The short cut showed the neat roundness of skull.

'You wanted to talk to her, this evening.'

'I had to see her. Always putting things off, putting me off! It's the man whom she was seeing, no doubt of that.'

'Who was this, Mr Sharpe?'

'I don't know,' he said quickly. 'How could I know, without following her about, watching her house? Hardly dignified or reasonable, that. There was someone. Leading me on until something more attractive turned up. Damnable! You see she could not be allowed to get away with that. A cold woman. Basically cold, calculating, and an outward show all charm, complaisance. Would you believe that I thought her the sweetest woman I had ever met? Sweet!' and he slammed both fists on the back of the chair beside him. 'Claire Fairlie was a bitch, a heartless bitch who would lead men on and throw them over. Perhaps he found her out. She was almost kind, spoke of using me badly. I think she was trying to placate me. Yes, trying to placate me, no doubt of that. I had frightened her. She realised what intensity she had provoked. I said she had come to a reckoning. I warned her we were at the end. That I would end it. She agreed that we must talk. There is no doubt that the threat frightened her. This room is always stifling. Unbearable.' He stepped to the hearth and turned off the electric fire, and stood like a paterfamilias on the hearthrug. 'I didn't kill her. I did not. Emphatically not. I don't deny that I have wanted to or even dreamt of it, but the horror—the horror of finding her there like that. Like that!' He covered his face, fingertips pressing his eyes. Then he drew his hands down and lifting his chin said, 'I find I am giving way to hysteria. I've not been myself since that damnable woman first—you must see a great many people in a great variety of states of distress, and no doubt look at them all with the same receptive non-committal calm. Wait until you've been through something yourself. That's all. You may find out what is at the bottom of all the hysteria, that it is real and genuine feeling.'

'Anyone who reaches middle life without suffering must be either abnormally lucky or abnormally thick-skinned,' said Bone. His voice was measured after the staccato of Mr Sharpe. He looked at the man: the conventional clothes, of whose shocking stains he seemed unconscious; the repressive closing of the mouth, the lower lip tightened so that small lines sprang up either side of his chin; the round orbs of eyes capped by lids whose heaviness gave him a rather insolent stare. An egotist, plausible, clever, probably capable of violence and also of so convincing himself of justification that he could not so much act innocence as believe himself innocent. This was an ability more common than any pre-Freudian would have credited.

Bone sat on the end of the desk and said, 'Mr Sharpe, can you give me a chronological account of your movements from the beginning of the opera tonight?'

Sharpe put his hands together and tapped the forefingers to his mouth. He came to sit in one of the tall-backed chairs.

'I was stationed at the side of the stage. To keep order among those waiting to go on. There are only curtains across the front of the wings—but you will have noticed that—and any disturbance can be heard by the audience. I volunteered for the task, since unlike some of my colleagues I can keep order. There was an extra incentive, in that I hoped—expected —to see Claire. As producer she had always stood on the side of the stage I chose, but she evaded me, perhaps deliberately. I found that she had elected to work from the other side. I did see her, however. There is just room behind the backcloth for a man of my build to edge across. There were, of course, others at the prompt side as well.'

'What others, Mr Sharpe? Who were they?'

Sharpe, intent on his narrative, flicked an irritable hand. 'Mrs Lambert and a prefect. I don't know the prefect's name, she doesn't take German, but she is foreign. Well, I spoke to Claire. I insisted that she should make time to talk to me. She agreed that she would. I returned to my post. Apart from that I did not see her until . . . after the performance. I had been shocked at the arrival of that girl, that—' his head turned as if he sought the name, from left to right—'Beverly Braun. To see her come on instead of Claire and give that astonishing, that vulgar display! At the rehearsal Claire's interpretation had been restrained, a little roguish, but quite in keeping. I could hardly contain myself. I could not think why she had allowed such a thing to take place. As soon as the last scene was in progress I went round to the far side. Claire was not to be seen. For the first time I understood that she was actually missing. It

32

was not until they hooked open the doors from the stage that I saw the bolt at the top of her dressing-room door. I unlocked it with no expectation, supposing that others would have seen it before and looked in. The lights were on. At first I did not see her. Then—' he spread his hands briefly and then ducked his head. He pulled out a handkerchief and clasped it to his mouth. After a moment he looked up. 'That is all I can tell you. I'm not entirely certain of what happened, of what I did, after I saw her.'

'Thank you, Mr Sharpe. What were you hoping for in talking to Miss Fairlie? What did you want to establish?'

'What?' He stared, then lifted his chin fractionally and gazed straight ahead. 'Our relationship.'

'Which was?'

He sat rigid.

Bone pursued with detached calm. 'What was your relationship?'

'We had been lovers.'

The tone was final, as though he expected nothing more to be said. Bone thrust from his mind incongruous pictures of this pedantic inhibited man as a lover, and said, 'Had been, Mr Sharpe? When?'

'It was not recent. It was apparently over.'

'When?'

He was not proof against Bone's silent waiting. His eyes were wide and he sat as if fastened to the chair. His underlip suddenly twitched. 'In the summer. Last term. And the start of September. Then she began to put me off. To evade. She was charming as ever.' He chopped the word contemptuously. 'Just before half-term she seemed to be renewing the affaire. Then it was over in fact although she pretended . . . we dined together. She would not discuss the future. Then lately she once again seemed much warmer. Much . . .' and his body trembled with tension. 'Must we go on with this? It's intolerable.'

Bone was initiating an inner discussion between common sense and gut feeling when Locker eased his big frame silently round the door and crossed the room.

'Right greenhouse in here,' Locker muttered. 'Sir, we've got word among the girls of someone looking in at the back.

And you'll recollect the complaints yesterday, no Friday, and this morning about a man hanging around outside schools.'

An outsider and a Peeping Tom.

Bone stood up. 'Let's hear about this,' he said. 'Mr Sharpe, would you wait here?'

Locker said, 'They've got cups of tea going.'

'We'll send you a cup of tea.'

'That would be very welcome. Thank you.'

The man probably needed a brandy more than tea. He was blowing his nose, and had just discovered the state of his clothes, looking at them with birdlike turns of the head over his handkerchief. Outside, Bone said, 'I don't want to let him leave, but at the moment I find him convincing. Can we have a man in the Hall here, please?'

'They're ready to take away the body. Do you want to—'

'No, they can do that.'

'I'll send someone along.'

Bone stood in the entrance hall. There was a shield with the school crest, which he was used to seeing on Charlotte's blazer, and dark oak panels with names of University scholars who had been at the school. Also, below the crest, was a shorter panel with head girls' names. It must be pleasant to see your daughter's name here. Several appeared on both lists. He did not imagine Charlotte as University material. She had lost too much schooling, she was not a scholar by nature.

P.C. Clifford arrived, and Bone after a word with him headed for the dressing-rooms to the left of the stage.

A man had certainly been seen looking in from the play-ground. The girls had in fact Sellotaped newspaper over the lower panes. One girl averred it was Harry Birch, but others argued that he was too indistinct. He had first appeared close to, but then had stood farther off in the dark.

Bone was frustrated over questioning Prue. Her parents were both away. Mrs Grant was a social worker, and was on a course, Paul Grant was in Wales on business, trying to find a source for a component his works needed. There was difficulty in getting in touch with either; and although Bone was a family friend he was not going to risk trouble. Charlotte said that Mrs Shaw, the Biology teacher, had said she would run them home, and he sent them both off. Charlotte, as she went, gave him her singular, glowing smile. He was fortified.

The Hall's lights had been diminished, so that it seemed larger. From the D.S. side came sounds of voices in valedictory mode. Bone paused at the entrance door, looking down the perspective given by opened side curtains and swing doors, to where Locker was sealing the D.S. room. He sent his voice at a low carrying pitch: 'Miss Mallett's room, Steve.'

Locker acknowledged, and Bone passed through the entrance hall. A desultory clatter came from the basement, otherwise all was quiet. Now Bone paused to look at what he thought of Sharpe. He had been deliberately thinking of other things while he let his opinion of the real subject brew. In Sharpe he had a man of authority. A limited sphere of authority certainly, but a man who could say 'Come' and 'Go' and be obeyed, a phenomenon by no means as common among teachers as one might expect. Now, having made his statement, he would expect it to be believed; Bone, personally, was inclined to believe it. He did not think Sharpe would abscond if in fact he were guilty, because the man would see no reason to do so. If Bone let him go and he was guilty and did take off for foreign parts, Bone's head would be on a platter, with the Chief Constable as a formidable Salome. Try to arrange to have a watch on him.

He sent Clifford in search of a cup of tea and went into the room. It seemed no less hot, and Sharpe was in shirtsleeves, one cuff rimmed with red-brown. He pulled himself more upright in the chair. He seemed unsurprised at being allowed to go, and not particularly relieved.

'Do you live alone?' Bone asked him, as he was getting into his stained jacket.

'Yes. I have rooms here. My home is in Guildford, but it proved far too much of a journey. Far too much, even with the M.25.'

'Advice from an old campaigner,' Bone said. 'Don't do without a meal tonight.'

Sharpe stared, then finished pulling his jacket on and said 'Quite. I don't want one, but I shall need one. Quite.' At the door he said, 'Thank you.'

Bone's remark had been prompted, perhaps, by his own hunger. At this moment, Clifford opened the door to Mrs Lambert who, followed by Locker, was bearing a tray with, besides tea, a plate of assorted biscuits, slices of cake, and sausage rolls.

'That's very welcome, Mrs Lambert.'

She came forward to put the tray on the desk, a slender woman in a yellow skirt and the school pullover she had been wearing before. Her reddish-brown hair stood out, like an overgrown short-crop, round a thin face showing strain. It was a face of dramatic cheekbones and deep eyes. Locker, by a mime consisting of riffling his notebook, waving a negative hand above it and pointing at Mrs Lambert, conveyed that he had not talked to her. Bone stood behind one of the armchairs, therefore, offering it to her. He helped himself to tea and a biscuit; he would have preferred a sausage roll, but was wary of puff pastry. It has a marked ability to disperse itself over the immediate landscape, which is not consonant with much dignity. He took the other armchair, slightly against his instinctive wish to dominate by staying on his feet. She refused tea. She had had some. She sat with her feet tucked to one side, her clasped hands on one thigh, turning slightly away from Bone with her body, tentatively answering his put-them-at-ease smile.

'We're trying to sort out exactly what was happening all evening, Mrs Lambert. You were on the prompt side of the stage, is that right?'

'Yes. I was.'

'Were you there all evening?'

Her voice was first inaudible, then abrupt. 'I'm sorry. . . . Such a strain. A mercy so many of the girls had gone before . . . discovered . . . Yes, I was there all evening except that once or twice things were wanted. Fazileh is a very able prefect, though. She stands no nonsense.'

Bone said, 'So you had competent help in keeping order. Mrs Lambert, would you very much mind if I took off my coat? Miss Mallett keeps this room very warm.'

'She taught in Africa, and she says that her blood is still thin. We are all used to it. I feel quite cold, as it happens.' She gave a nervous little laugh. 'It's shock, I think. I don't feel hot

36

at all. Quite cold. I've felt cold ever since . . . this jersey was on the side of the stage. The girls leave everything everywhere and I simply co-opted it.'

Shock was a curious thing, Bone thought, that a person could feel cold and yet be sweating.

'When was the last time you actually saw Miss Fairlie?'

CHAPTER
4

'Well, everybody was everywhere, of course. It's so hard to say. I believe she said she was going to make up now, I heard her say that, but I don't know what was going on at the time, on the stage I mean. She had been watching, encouraging people, you know. She was everywhere of course. As to when I last saw her,' and she made a curious sound, a catch in the breath between a gasp and a laugh, 'when you said that I thought of when I actually did last see her, but you meant when she was alive.'

'Could you see the door of the Domestic Science room from where you were stationed?' He knew the answer to this one.

'Not all the time, and not at all well. The swing doors have glass in the top, but we kept that corridor in darkness as the lights showed through. It's not a satisfactory theatre at all. Miss Fairlie was trying to get alterations made, but so far Miss Mallett has not persuaded the Governors.'

'And other people? Whom did you see on your side, apart from the girls who were acting, and the prefect?'

'Miss Dunne came round once. Mr Sharpe, who should have been on the other side, he was there. He came through the doors and went behind the back scenery. Of course he is quite slight, but I was surprised that he could get through there. Before the play began, Miss Wallace was to and fro all the time, and she bobbed in once or twice after. I'm sure it distracted the audience seeing her go to and fro, and I finally was really firm about it. She was taking belongings through to the girls at first, and then messages from their parents and so on. She likes to be useful, but well ... She is very good-natured.'

'When did you see Mr Sharpe coming out of the doors?'

'Let me see. It was when all the girls were on stage doing their dance. Two of them have a fight, and they talk about stealing, and they sing and then dance. It's quite pretty, but considering what they are supposed to be, I'm surprised their parents don't mind. Some of them are not very decently dressed.'

'Before a private audience,' Bone said, 'it's different, surely.' Her primness was a little surprising. 'What happened when Miss Fairlie could not be found?'

'I sent round to the other side to see if she was there when the girls first told me she was missing. They said she was not in the D.S. room; they had been outside and looked through the window. But of course she could not be seen.' Mrs Lambert brought her hands up rather like an Indian salutation, and sighed. 'Someone suggested that she might be in the staffroom or lavatory. I thought it hardly likely, but I went to see.'

'Would she not have had to come through the Hall to reach it?'

'I had to go out that way, certainly. *She* might have gone outdoors and in through the side door. The girls pointed that out—she was so much against any disturbance in the Hall, of people going to and fro. But my looking was all a waste of time. As it happened.'

The remark was a slightly odd one. He said, 'What friends and foes had Miss Fairlie among the staff?'

'Friends and—? She hadn't any close friends. I think most of her friends were out of school; she knew a good many of the parents socially, I believe. It was thought that she and Mr Sharpe were engaged at one time, but neither of them said so, although there was talk behind their backs. That was last summer. From his behaviour he is still very taken with her. Was. One can't realise ... I don't think she had any foes. We have our quarrels, as people do who work together. Miss Fairlie was apt to get passions for causes, or on behalf of some girl she felt was not getting a fair deal. We were used to that.'

Bone let the silence go on, and held his enquiring face. She

said, 'It could be irksome, but of course these things ... No.'
She was not to be drawn into committing herself further.

Claire Fairlie's locker contained a box of coffee-bags, a tin of crispbread, a plastic box full of cheap jewellery labelled with small tags of girls' names (confiscations, said Miss Mallett) and her handbag, a blue pochette in pleated ciré leather. In this, house keys, tissues, one clean and one with lipstick; a compact of cream powder; two lipsticks, one pink and one orange; a small comb; a red biro; a notebook, quite new, with spelling lists and examples of apostrophe usage, and 'Props lent'.

'We'll get along to her house after this,' Bone said. He had been asking Miss Mallett about Claire Fairlie's friends and foes, with much the same result. 'I don't think, Superintendent, that any of the alliances and enmities in the staffroom were such as to lead to this conclusion.'

He thought, Something did, and one doesn't know.

A thin woman with wild hair burst in from the hall and, holding the door-handle as if she needed support, cried, 'Miss Mallett, what do we do with—oh!'

'Yes, Miss Wallace. Come in. What's the matter?'

Miss Wallace seemed to find her height a disadvantage. She rounded her shoulders and shrank in upon herself. Protuberant blue eyes moved swiftly, with faint acknowledgement of Locker, who must have interviewed her, faint alarm at Bone, apology to Miss Mallett.

'It's the *flowers*, Headmistress. The thank-you flowers for Miss Fairlie. So expensive. Lying there in the lab. What do we do with them?'

Probably the same thought was suppressed in several minds: they won't last for the funeral.

'I shall take them to the hospital, Miss Wallace. How thoughtful of you to remind me. In the Physics lab? Thank you.'

Miss Wallace fluttered, ducked, and took the door-handle safely out into the entrance hall.

'An able physicist,' said Miss Mallett blandly. 'Excellent with the younger children. A most conscientious woman.'

As Bone said goodbye to Miss Mallett he was struck by her Rock of Ages look. Headmistresses must sail through storms, to change the metaphor, unchanging, like figureheads; though he could not imagine Miss Mallett's hair, under any circumstances, being blown back. No indecorous *Cutty Sark* for her; to think of that was to envisage Lady Bracknell in a mini-skirt. No strain showed on her face. He wondered how this event would affect the school.

Locker came with him to Claire Fairlie's house. Bone, who was tired, welcomed this. As they got out of the car in the quiet street they both paused: a grumble of thunder had sounded, like a dramatic cue.

'When I was a kid,' Locker said, 'we only got thunder in summer, after a good long hot spell at that. Now they can fix it for us even at Christmas.'

'That's democracy for you.' Fat drops were falling as they trod up the steps. A light glowed behind red curtains in the basement. The Ingersoll key unlocked the front door.

Before Bone could find the hall light he was unpleasantly brushed by a hanging plant, and the switch illuminated a little brown-walled hall filled with jungle.

'Kew Gardens,' Locker said. Spider plants, ferns, a yucca fancying itself in a long mirror by the hat-stand, where a long mac, never to be worn again, dropped over the plant-pot at the base. From this pot ivy sprouted, climbing strings towards the top.

'What you reckon happens when there's lots of coats there?'

'Ivy can pull a house down. Bit of tweed won't upset it.' Bone thought of the woman who had stepped along this hall today to meet a knife. When she watered these plants she would not have thought it was for the last time. A last time for everything, just as when I realised at school that I'd played my last game of football. Mostly you don't know, and it's as well.

The living-room stopped them both inside the door. Painted bright orange as to walls and ceiling, it had Times Furnishing reproduction Jacobean furniture, dark, shining with varnish, all curlicues and bulbous legs. One small table and a chair had been painted, imperfectly, white, but Claire Fairlie evidently gave up after that. There were African violets, a fern, two pots of chrysanthemums, one of them, against good sense and safety, on the television. A video set stood next to it with the red light vigilantly glowing. The table, piled with papers and books, had ringmarks in plenty and a half-empty coffee mug, whose fluid carried a viscous film.

'Report forms,' said Bone. 'Beverly Braun's terrific sense of fun makes her an asset to the class. Less fantasy and more factual description would give her essays variety.' He looked across at Locker. 'Meaning she's difficult to nail down to anything, from the sound of it, and is a pest in lessons. Here's books to mark, essays. Letters.' There was plenty to do.

The video set buzzed, clicked, and began to record. They had both started. Now they looked at it and, after a moment, Bone stooped and pressed the stop switch. We make things ready, we trust the future without thinking. A list, headed 'cards' and 'prezzies', lay next to the report form. Some of the names were ticked.

'Let's take a quick dekko round. Detail later.'

Accordingly, Locker went up the stairs. They ascended straight from the living room, a wall having evidently been taken down to give this extra space. Bone opened a door at the rear into a kitchenette, little more than a cupboard. Instant coffee, crispbread, an empty milk bottle; nail varnish, a hairbrush. Bone touched nothing.

A door under the stairs opened and a young man appeared behind a pot of flowers.

'Oh sorry. Thought it was Claire.' He had second, visible thoughts. 'You're not *burglars*, are you?' Was it a coy hope succeeding the fear? 'I thought from the footsteps it was Claire. You *are* light on your feet, aren't you? Heard a man go upstairs, *not* unusual, but you've real fairy footsteps. Is Claire here?'

Bone was aware of being sized up, of feelers delicately extended. At sight of a warrant card the young man, but he was not quite as young as at first glance, gave a small lively yelp. Then he sobered. 'Is she all right? Has there been an accident?'

'Yes. I'm sorry.'

'How bad?'

'Miss Fairlie is dead.'

He put down the pot with a thud on the fridge and subsided

onto the kitchen stool. He had gone white and the small lines showed. 'Oh God. Oh dear, such a lovely lady too. And so kind. Sometimes it seems to happen only to nice people. What was it? Car accident?'

'No, not an accident. Someone killed her.'

'Killed. You mean ... But ... can't believe anyone could possibly want to hurt her. I do feel odd. Can't stand even the thought of ... I say, there's brandy in that cupboard.'

'I'm sorry. It shouldn't be touched.'

'Oh. No. What a terrible way to go. Suppose really there isn't a nice way, come to think. Not sure I wouldn't rather get it between the shoulder-blades sooner than peg out by smelly degrees like an old pug; or in hospital.'

Locker had heard voices and now looked over the banister. He could move quietly when he chose. He came down and regarded, fascinated, the tears on the young man's cheeks.

'Really, don't think I can manage without a drink. Won't you come down to my flat?'

He stood up.

'Should say my name and number, shouldn't I? Edward Treasure, Teddy Treasure that is. You'll have guessed I live downstairs.'

The atmosphere was totally different once the basement door was open. Treasure clattered down the stairs as if cheered by the prospect of a drink, but he turned at the foot to peer up and make a hospitable gesture. They went down. A Beardsley picture of a woman at her dressing-table hung at the stair-head, and down the wall hung a row of plates. Bone saw with surprise a large smear of mustard on one and, on the next, a crust of bread appliqué'd. Teddy Treasure was evidently a joker. He had made a rather accurate guess at the method of killing, but the shock had looked genuine. Bone kept an open mind.

A smell of scent and baking bread welcomed them. The front room was painted white, with jade woodwork, scrupulously clean and tidy. A jade sofa-bed along one wall faced a very pretty *bonheur-du-jour*. Teddy had paused, and saw Bone looking at it.

'Yes, it *is* beyond my income bracket. I'm a partner in

Lofting Antiques. "Antiques"—' his forefingers put inverted commas in the air—'junk really, but everyone's upwardly mobile, aren't they, and I hope to be in antiques ere long.'

He gestured them through a plush indigo curtain into the kitchen. Pine and bamboo predominated here, and the neatness made Bone wonder how he had got on with the disorganised Claire. There was, however, another object in the kitchen, a large pantherine young man almost flat on his back in a wicker chair.

'This is Merc Quinn. M.E.R.C. For Mercator's Projection, you know. Oh mustn't,' said Teddy, and slapped the back of his own hand. Merc raised his eyes and made no other move. Like Teddy he wore the uniform: trainers, dark trousers, white tee-shirt, denim jacket, but his tee-shirt was plain while Teddy's sported a pop-star face. Merc, with prune-dark eyes, strong bones, and heavy dark moustache bracketing his mouth's corners, resembled the singer Freddy Mercury, which might be the origin of his name, but his hair, unlike his moustache and sleek eyebrows, was flax blond.

'It's the police, Merc.' Teddy's tone had changed. 'Claire, Claire's been killed. It's awful. Murdered.'

Merc did not react. Bone supposed that if told 'I've come to arrest you for it,' the man might refuse to move. The glance he allowed to drift over Bone and Locker suggested, if anything, that the police were responsible for the whole thing.

The room was oppressively warm. Bone, sliding out of his mac, thought he was going, today, from one hothouse to another. There was another little yelp from Teddy as the oven-timer pinged, and he bent to take out a tray of bread-rolls from the oven. Merc came to life like a large cat at the sight of Whiskas.

Teddy busied himself getting plates, butter and knives. As he dried a knife, he deftly tipped from a half-bottle of brandy on the shelf into a cup, and drank it off. The tilt of the bottle as he poured implied that this was all there was.

Merc had transferred himself to a bamboo stool by the table, with economy of movement, and let himself be served. Treasure waited on him, giving a little admiring push as he bit into the hot bread, as if to say 'He can put it all back by himself,

44

doesn't need any help.' The teeth, beautiful and white, did not measure up to Freddy Mercury's splendid array, which Charlotte declared to be so sexy.

Bone refused an indigestible hot roll. Locker took one with alacrity, despite a side glance from Merc of jealous disapproval. It was a wonder Merc did not growl.

Treasure, upset by Bone's refusal, ferreted in the cupboard and produced a tin.

'Home-made treacle biscuit? Oh do. Good.' The coffee had now percolated and he poured. Bone, provided against his wishes with a cup, held it and waited to speak. Teddy did not eat. He said, 'It seems so awful, doesn't it? I can't take it in. Poor Claire. I know life just has to go on, regardless, but you forget. All that year Dad was dying I simply ate and ate. Came back from the hospital and ate like a pig. He was on a drip, you know. And I kept thinking ooh, before I get like that I must have another pizza. Put on a stone that year. It really was wretched. Then I met Merc and he helped.'

Bone speculated on how Merc could have achieved this. Hardly by consoling talk. Perhaps by assisting with the eating.

'It's not known who?' Teddy asked delicately.

'Not as yet.'

'You'll want to know about her friends,' Teddy nodded. Bone had taken a mouthful of coffee. Warm, sharp, stimulating, it coursed down his throat. He ate the biscuit. He had been hungry and now realised it. Teddy, while talking, put the tin within reach. 'Of course she had so many friends. Seems weird to be saying "had". She changed her boyfriend lately. It used to be Ian. Madly uptight little man with nerves all overtuned. For some reason took a scunner at me and wanted Claire to give us the boot. She thought that was very funny. I rather think she thought this Ian was very funny after a bit. So intense, he was.'

'Has he been here lately?'

'No. When was the last time Ian was in the house, Merc? I don't think since October. It's not that I'm a Paul Pry, but living down here we can hear voices, you know, and if Claire was talking from the kitchen to someone in the front you'd hear more. Even not *listening* you'd just be *aware*. Now it's

45

Michael. Money, and very smooth, and I've seen him around the town. Claire hasn't said. About him, I mean. Don't know why I think he's married and I may be wrong. Claire talks quite freely, I mean she knows she can, to us. I'm discreet and Merc's not a gossip.'

He paused at this understatement to ensure that Merc had enough butter. 'Then there was Martin. He came for coaching for his A-levels but he was terribly *épris* with Claire. She was a teentsy bit naughty, boys that age have such strong feelings. I said to her "You don't *know*, Claire." We got to know him when she was late one day. Pouring with rain, and we heard someone ring and then wait, stamping about on the step, so I went out and looked up, there he was getting soaked, so we asked him in.'

Bone wondered what part Merc had played in thus inviting Martin in. Most probably this was Martin Grant, Prue's brother.

'A really nice boy. Very interesting. He and Merc got on so well, didn't you? They've both got this fascination with mediaeval Japan.'

Bone experienced a convulsion of disbelieving laughter at his diaphragm. He could trust his face, and he looked at Merc with nothing but polite question. 'Have you indeed?' he said.

Merc put his knife quietly across his plate and got to his feet. Locker's head went back, looking up as Merc rose and rose. This action in itself, Bone thought, constituted threatening behaviour.

'You're not late, are you?' Teddy asked. 'Merc goes to the club tonight.'

Merc stepped past Locker, took a well-cared-for leather coat off the back of the door and, with unaltered and therefore brooding face, blew them all a kiss, and went.

'He's got such style!' Teddy said as the door shut.

'Is he going to a club at this hour?'

'He helps them to close.'

Bone had a fantasy of Merc on a pale horse, helping God to close on the last day. 'I see. What other friends had Miss Fairlie?'

'Oh *tons*. Girls from the school often dropped in. She was so sweet with them. You'd think school hours'd be enough but

46

she really gave them her time. Not many *women* friends. She would dine out quite often with couples she knew. Then there was another man before Ian but that was when I first came, just after her father emigrated, and I didn't know him.'

'Where did Mr Fairlie emigrate to?'

'Or-strye-lyer. For the climate. He liked the sun. There'll be his address in her part of the house somewhere. Oh poor man, he'll have to know. She used to write to him quite often. She'd say when we told her a story, "I must put that in my next to Dad." She'd an aunt and an uncle in the north, perhaps Scotland, and a married sister too. Claire was from Scotland, though to hear her you wouldn't know. Oh, I can't believe she's gone. And who'd kill her? She was lovely, such a lovely lady.'

'Can you think of anyone who did not like her?'

'I can't. Can't *imagine* any, even. I'm not saying she couldn't be quick-tongued sometimes. And she'd say something funny, for instance, that was quite hurtful. And made fun about some of the teachers in her school, but that's just a way of talk, isn't it? She used to imitate them till we rolled about laughing.'

Bone began to surmise that Teddy's 'we' was himself alone. Even a brief acquaintance with Merc was enough to preclude the likelihood of several of the activities Teddy ascribed to him.

'She was always helping people. She had a very—oh what? —a moral sense, if you like. Not conventional, not moral like that. No, about helping people. Love your neighbour and that.'

Bone put down his cup and said, 'You've been very helpful, Mr Treasure. I expect we shall ask you more. For the moment, however . . .'

Treasure came to the foot of the stairs with them. 'Anything I can tell you. Anything I can do. Still can't realise.' He put his fingers to his mouth. 'I suppose we'll have to leave here. Oh dear.'

'All these things take time,' Bone said, 'and tenants have rights too. Goodnight.'

Upstairs they looked through the place, gathered up all the address books, diaries, pass-book from Lloyd's Bank, letters, cards, and went though about a quarter of it. Bone said, 'The rest tomorrow, Steve. It's bloody late. I'm tired, you're tired, your wife will be cursing me.'

Locker handed him, using fingertips only, a piece of blue writing paper. 'This was in the brown handbag,' he said. Bone bent to read it. The writing was bold and scrawled.

You've ruined everything for me. You think you needn't bother about me, that I don't matter. I'll show you you're wrong. *I promise you* I'll show you what I can do.

M.

CHAPTER
5

They discussed, in the car, the possibilities of the M as Martin, or Michael, or even Merc ('though it's not his *style*').

'I expect,' Locker said, ducking his head in again as he left, 'it's Miss Mallett.'

Bone snapped his fingers: of course! and they exchanged tired grins as Locker shut the door.

The streets were empty. Lights dazzled and swam on the glisten of tarmac, the wipers monotonously swung. His mind went on over the faces seen, the voices heard, the oddnesses of look, of tone, Sharpe's volcanic hysteria, the suppression in Mrs Lambert. They had gone over the people Locker had seen, staff and girls. More people to be seen tomorrow. We have so little perception of what goes on in the heads of others. Some liars watch for the effect of what they say, others are sublimely confident, absorbed in a story they almost believe. It is a wonder that any conversation at all makes sense when you consider the deserts that exist between one mind and another.

He stopped outside his door and knew his depression for fatigue.

He put his key in the lock. Bone weary, he thought. It was hard coming to an empty house, and he wished he had not sent Charlotte to Prue's. Even though at this hour she'd be in bed, there would have been her presence in the place. He shut the door on the lamplit street, and climbed the stairs, past the offices on the first floors, putting lights on ahead of him and off downstairs. It was a trudge, but top floors were less expensive.

He thought *someone's there*, and stopped, head tilted up. Cha, in pyjamas, leant over the balustrade on the landing. At her shin level, the grey marbled head of her young cat peered through too. She was smiling cheekily. The cat merely showed interest.

'I thought—'

'But I wanted to see you. Hated you coming to an empty place. I'll put the kettle on.'

The heads were withdrawn. Cha's uneven scamper, the soft gallop of Ziggy, crossed the landing. He was grinning, he found, as he took off his jacket. The kitchen, with the blue jar of gold chrysanthemums, glowed. She turned from the stove.

'Now what for supper, Pa? Bacon and eggs.'

'At this hour? Cha, that could not sound better if you set it to music.'

She broke out into 'Bacon and eggs' to the tune she had sung in the Opera, and the freedom of her singing voice, and her wit, and her care, made him go over and hug her. She hugged him fiercely in return. He was home.

'But you had no business to be here, chick, you understand? I don't like you alone in the house.'

'No. You would want no supper. I don't like you alone in here too.'

'You mustn't get worried over me. I'm old enough to mess up my own life; anyway I gave someone good advice about being sure to have a meal whether it was wanted or not, only this evening.'

'Who?'

'That's shop.'

They sat down, across the table from each other. She had the young cat on her knee, her feet on a stretcher of the table. She poured tea. She was wide awake.

'Lucky it's not much in the way of lessons at this tag-end of term,' he said. 'You'll be flaked tomorrow.'

'You look flaked right now.'

'Nothing bacon and eggs won't cure, with a bit of sleep.'

'Mrs Garland says they're indigestible together. It's the albumen.'

Bone's reply was to fork some more albumen into his mouth. He said after a moment, 'How is Prue?'

'I think she's all right. She told me all about what she'd seen, this weird noise, so she pushed the D.S. door and looked round and there was Mr Sharpe holding Miss Fairlie, sort of hugging and lifting her, and he was crying. It was an awful noise, and she saw blood all on the floor, and he was saying her name and "Darling" and things, so she pulled the door shut and Miss Dunne was coming, so she said "Something's happened, something awful" and *she* looked and said "Send Fazileh for Miss Mallett at once" and went in.'

Bone reflected that he was getting the benefit of Prue's evidence although he could not use it. The effect so far was to corroborate Sharpe. Nevertheless, the man might still have put the knife away and gone back to the body to weep at what he had done. A scenario for this wrote itself busily in Bone's mind.

'Daddy.'

'M'm?'

'Eat. You're thinking.'

'How popular was Miss Fairlie?'

'Mad-ly, with some. She had faves, n'she dropped them.'

This last word was a recent accomplishment of Cha's and came very clearly. After the crash he had been told that she might not regain articulate speech. His inarticulate daughter crammed bacon into her mouth and, after a short chew, went on: 'People were bats over her or couldn't stand. But not bad enough to kill! She would help a lot, go out of her way for people. She could be mean. I heard Bev Braun say "Don't ask *me* to get things from Sugar Plum, I'm *yesterday's* pet." ' Cha still said 'hings' for 'things' seven times out of ten. He noticed such matters sometimes; once he had been the sole decipherer of her speech. 'Wasn't Bev fantastic as Mrs Trapse? We all watched. Sharpie paid us no mind, he was staring like he'd never get his eyes back in again, and talking to himself.'

'Saying what?'

'Couldn't hear for the singing. Then he saw us and hooshed us all back into the rooms. Kat Hazeley said Sugar had eloped with her dad.' Bone kept his eyes on his plate at this. Charlotte pursued, 'Some girls said she was lezzie.'

'On what evidence?'

'Cos she was so sweet to some girls.'

'Hence the "Sugar Plum"?'

'Oh that was from Lou Reed. A song. "Walk on the Wild Side".'

Bone couldn't remember it, but the association was with iffy lyrics and the rather urgent degeneracy of a few years ago which he'd come in contact with over a youth-club scandal.

'All drug-and-drag?'

'Yeah, man. That's, like, *yesterday's* cool.'

This was the first case he had ever discussed with Cha. Was this a discussion? Could he prevent her, in any case, from knowing about it? Could he neglect a valid source of information? 'Will they ask you, tomorrow, if I've asked you?'

'Oh Daddy never discusses cases at home.'

'How much do you mind, chick?'

'About discussing cases?'

'About this one?'

'I didn't know her. She was just a person around school. It isn't like usual. I suppose, well, I suppose in fact it's almost exciting. That's not nice, is it?'

'It's normal.'

'I mean, a murder right at school. And you talking to me about it, I like that. I feel I should feel more sorry. A person dead, you feel you should like them and be sorry. It must have been terrible for her.'

'People who have survived stab wounds say it feels like a punch or a thump, darling. She wouldn't know it had happened.'

'Really? Not so bad, exactly.'

He put the plates in the washing-up bowl and ran water in. 'Bed. No more tonight.'

Cha, standing up and stretching, said, 'Sugar Plum. You never knew where you were. She would start a plan and Miss Dunne would finish it. Miss Dunne did rehearsals a lot for the Opera, but the programme said Producer, Miss Fairlie.'

Ziggy jumped onto Charlotte's warm chair and began to wash. They shut the doors and toiled upstairs to bed.

Bone woke what seemed two minutes later to the telephone's double shriek. Picking up his bedside extension, eyes still shut, he gave the number.

'Mr Bone—' a girl's voice. He took a deep breath to wake himself, knew the voice and said, 'Prue?'

'Mr Bone, Martin hasn't been in. I'm sorry to bother you. You sound awfully sleepy, did I wake you?'

'It's the right time for me to wake anyway. Of course you were right to call me. Where are your parents?'

'Daddy's up in Wales. Mummy's at this course. She'll be furious. She only went because we'd be together, and now he's not here; I'm worried sick because he had this thing about Miss Fairlie.'

'You get breakfast and get to school and don't worry. I'll phone around and get hold of the young rascal. Martin won't have done anything wild, you know. He most likely has been up on the Rocks having a drama, abiding the pelting of the pitiless storm.'

'I thought, you know, but hospitals, suppose he got knocked down.'

'I thought of that. I'll find out. I'll be at the school later and I'll see that you hear as soon as I find out.'

He got out of bed, organising reluctant arms and legs, carrying his dazed head to the bathroom. Brutal and blessed, cold water restored him to the world. Shaved and dressed, he went down and fed Ziggy, who walked on his feet all the time he was getting out the tin and opening it up. He put coffee on, then wrote a note and propped it on Charlotte's breakfast cup. *Please excuse my daughter Charlotte's lateness this morning. She was awake very late last night. R.D. Bone.* He put Ziggy's used Kittetray in its plastic bag into the bin and put out a new one, drank his coffee and, his chores done, put on his mac and left. The day was fresh and cool. An aery voice called him: Charlotte, at her window, waving. He blew a kiss, aware he could not do it with Merc's style.

Harry Birch unlocked the school gates. There were always some girls here even at this hour. They couldn't be that eager for lessons. He watched them walk over to the cloakroom entrance. One with a nice pair of legs and a nice fat bum, her skirt flipped under the bum at every step. Too bad they'd cracked down on the split skirts last year. You could see the inside thigh then when the girls walked. You could get hot, thinking. Wearing a skirt like that showed you that they wanted it. But they were teases, all right.

He shut the door of his workroom and fed the boiler, adjusting its input for 'day'; the clock was supposed to do that, but one of the staff, when they had a weekend course nobody had told him about, had barged in here and broken the tappet trying to turn the heating up. Lot of interfering bitches. The teapot sat on the boiler and he poured out his third cup and climbed onto the tall stool with its shiny dun-coloured cushion. He had got it when they threw out the old lab furniture. It was just the thing. Sitting on it, sipping, and quietly massaging his thigh, he watched the long window on the staircase and the climbing legs. Today he was going to Miss Mallett to withdraw his notice. He had the day in front of him. He was not under threat any more. A deep sense of comfort and peace pervaded him.

Miss Mallett, surveying the timetable, had telephoned her old friend Brenda Winant and asked if she could come in for the few days left of term. 'Our dreadful little tragedy is in the newspapers,' she said, her tone impassive. Brenda understood that things had to be faced in a certain way. 'You see why we need you; but if you feel the association to be unpleasant—'

'Nonsense, Cecilia. Of course I'll come.'

There were the local editors who had agreed that the girls should not be interviewed, but others might not be so amenable. Miss Dare was at the school gates fending off a reporter now, and the policeman at the gate seemed disposed to help her. So far, Mr Sharpe had not rung up, so perhaps he was coming in. He had been very distressed. To come today would be brave of him. Though he was a sensitive man, he had backbone. It was to be hoped he would come.

She picked up her hymn book and Bible, with their markers in place, and walked to the door as the bell for Assembly rang. As so often, she recalled her old Headmistress at this point, stalking, stately, in her gown, the pince-nez buttoned to her navy frock on that fascinating cord with its spring-lock. The school, through which an eager, studious Cecilia Mallett had progressed, used to watch as she drew out the cord, installed the pince-nez, read the notices, took off the pince-nez and allowed the fine cord to wind into the button. It was part of the soothing ritual of schooldays. Today she had to wrap up Claire Fairlie's fate in a soothing ritual for the girls. There were many absent. The telephone had been ringing all morning since eight o'clock: girls upset, parents shocked.

Julia Craven knocked at the door. The school had assembled. Miss Mallett emerged, acknowledged the Head Girl's 'Good morning,' and paced into Hall. Poor Claire. An able and inspiring teacher, a little too popular. I could have given her a good shake once or twice for trying to tell me my job, but the gracious snubs I actually gave were probably more effective. She would never have made a good Deputy. Poor girl! So vital, too. That was attractive. Yes, *nil nisi*. One must think of all that was attractive in her.

Mrs Garland was not in Assembly. She was applying arnica to Kat Hazeley's cheekbone. Kat, subdued, said she had walked into a door. They both recognised this time-hallowed excuse for the euphemism it was. Mrs Garland was particularly sorry to see that all this had started again, as for almost a year her father had not hit her. It was never systematic abuse nor continual cruelty. He would lash out at her. The matter had been brought up more than once at staff meetings, but Miss Mallett said that unless the child herself, at her age, seemed to be asking for help, outside interference would do more harm than good.

'There. Hold that to it, Kat.'

When the bell went for first lesson, none of the staff was very prompt to leave the staffroom. In contrast to the noise from the classrooms, the staff were very quiet, people avoiding each other's eyes. Some confabulation between two of the staff stopped rather obviously when Mr Sharpe came in. He looked round, contemptuously, and went out again. Mrs Lambert was not there, but often at this time of day she was with Miss Mallett.

Miss Wallace, alone, did not seem disturbed. She was placidly tidying her locker, being free first lesson. Nicola Garland tapped Mrs Shaw's arm and nodded towards Miss Wallace, who had tied a ribbon like an Alice band round her hair, with the bow on top, scarlet, festive. Nicola thought few things worse than a woman of forty in the hairstyle of fourteen.

Grizel Shaw leant back and, running her hand through her own cropped hair that made her look like a wicked choirboy, and speaking so that only Nicola could hear, said, 'Very funerary.'

Mr Sharpe arrived at his German class and rapped out as he entered, 'File paper. Vocabulary test.'

'But it's the last week of *term*!' Sarah Crouch exclaimed.

'Don't let yesterday's little triumph of Macheath go to your head,' said Mr Sharpe. 'This test was promised for last week, and when I allowed you all to go to a rehearsal I warned you that it would take place this week instead. Ready.'

Sarah hissed to Anita da Silva, 'He's had his moustache ironed.' He looked dapper, hard, and haggard.

'Hasn't slept,' Anita wrote on her rough-book. He began the test. After the fourth word, Caroline Dewitt flung up her hand.

'Yes?'

'What's happening about the German trip at New Year, sir? Who's coming instead of Miss Fairlie?'

'Cancelled. The trip is cancelled. Your parents will receive a refund.' The pencil he was holding suddenly cracked and splintered. He dropped it into the bin and gave the next word. As he walked down the aisle in his usual fashion, known as cheat-checking, several girls moved, perhaps involuntarily, avoiding a contact he certainly did not offer. Patsy Briggs, helplessly behind, hopeless at German, now burst into tears as usual.

'I warned you that one more of these silly displays would

mean detention. It will now, of course, be next term.' He took out a pocket diary, leafed through it, and came to stand over Patsy. 'It will be on the fifteenth.' He tapped her book. 'January the fifteenth.'

Patsy, weeping, wrote it down.

Anita da Silva wrote on her book, and pushed it towards Sarah: *Bet he's a lifer by then.*

Mrs Garland was having to give D.S. lessons wherever a room was available, as her room was shut until further notice and was rumoured to be awash with policemen. The secretary was still monotonously telephoning parents of girls from the Opera cast-list for permission to have their girls interviewed. Locker and Fredricks had begun, in Room Seven where the doxies had dressed, to talk to the first ones, while Miss Mallett sat at the staff desk looking through the day's post. Locker had feared that her presence might put a stopper on the girls' willingness to talk, and indeed one or two who burst in were distinctly cooled when they saw her, but she also interposed with the tongue-tied, making a small joke, creating an atmosphere of ease. Locker admired this without liking it. He wished she would leave them to him, and that he was not so daunted that he could not tell her so. He looked at the girl he was interviewing, correct in uniform, with a scrubbed shining face, and was not to know how she had looked last night in a low-cut bodice, raddled, elf-locked under a mob cap, with a blacked-out tooth.

Maths with Mrs Lambert. She had not been in Assembly, and Miss Mallett had sonorously given out the hymns instead. Charlotte, getting her calculator out of its case, thought back with approval, with a sense of rightness, to the way Miss Mallett had spoken to them all of what had happened yesterday, had spoken sensibly and kindly and above all without sentiment.

Mrs Lambert came in and fumbled with her books, only preventing a cascade to the floor by a sudden lunge at them. She looked pale, unwell, and moved nervously when Susan came in late, as if she expected an attack.

Grue, chewing her fingers, was worrying about Martin and had to be nudged to get her book ready. 'Spent all night hugging the cats,' she had said. 'They helped.' In Cha's opinion, Martin was a dead loss, leaving his sister alone all night after what had happened. She was annoyed Grue hadn't come to stay with her. If Martin had come home after all and found no one there, *he* could worry for a change.

Both girls jumped when Mrs Lambert asked Grue a question. Grue didn't know the answer, perhaps hadn't heard. Mrs Lambert passed impatiently on. She rarely questioned Charlotte, who felt Baa-Lamb probably didn't like to hear her talk; she was always more inarticulate when asked something suddenly.

'Your father said he'd let me know about Martin. Mummy will be wild. He went missing a couple of weeks ago until one in the morning and came home pissed. She was wild then. Nobody wants their own family landing up as case-work. Suppose Mum had to be Martin's social worker.'

Cha had read *Bleak House* that summer. She thought of Mrs Jellyby again; it wasn't the distant heathen but the local Deprived who occupied Mrs Grant. The argument was that Martin and Prue had so much, so many advantages that they ought to give up their mother to good works. It was all right being without a mother, Cha thought, you could bear it if you had to and if your father took care of you. She minded for Prue more than Prue seemed to mind for herself.

'Don't suppose they'd let her be, for her own son.'

'Stop whispering!' Mrs Lambert's voice was plangent and they stopped. Not for nothing was she called Lamb Chop along with Baa-Lamb.

Cha, writing busily, considered the fantasy she and Grue had as to Miss Mallett's lovers. She kept them in the book cupboard where, if you put your ear, they could be heard clamouring faintly. Lamb Chop was, of course, on drugs, which accounted for her mood changes and, incidentally, for her ducking behind cars. Obviously this morning she was needing a fix. Wally, the pusher, kept the stuff in the lab, where they had orgies every so often.

Cha and Grue knew, uneasily, that some girls in school did *try things*, were said to be *on something*. Cha had said nothing to her father as she knew nothing for sure. It all might be fantasy. Bev Braun was supposed to be one; she frightened Charlotte with her appearance and her sudden harsh-voiced remarks. It did not help that Bev had stopped some girls from imitating Cha, had told them they were ——ing slags and ——ing pigs.

A note came suddenly via Susan who had dropped her pen. She put one hand on Cha's desk as she bent to retrieve it, and the note remained as the hand withdrew. *Fuzz interviewing suspects in Room Seven. Is your dishy daddy here?*

Fazileh entered. Mrs Lambert whirled round to face the door as if, once more, she expected someone with a gun.

'Miss Mallett says would you read this to the class?' Fazileh had been about to go on, but Mrs Lambert took the note and read out—she always read in a chant—'Some girls who took part in the Opera are being asked to help the police during this morning. Any girl called will leave her lesson *quietly* and go to Hall without talking to anyone.'

'Like French orals,' Susan said, *sotto*, but not much, *voce*.

'Also,' Fazileh said, 'please may Prudence Grant go now?'

Bone, after a visit to the station, let himself into Claire Fairlie's house again. It was quiet, full of still air. As he did not like to see plants wilting, he resolved to give some of them water before he left. He opened the basement door gently and listened. No sound. Treasure presumably had left for his antique shop, Merc, if there, must be sleeping. The basement door was not locked, which annoyed him. He believed he had seen Steve turn the key and take it. If Treasure had a key, and had come up and nosed around, he was going to get a flea in his ear.

Nothing seemed to be disturbed. Coffee cup, reports, books, Christmas list. Letters and pass-book had all gone to the station.

In the kitchen, where he went to look for the waste bin, a cupboard door nearly caught him in the temple. On a shelf within, a gap where his eye remembered something tall had stood. Damn Treasure. He must have come up for a bottle. He must have his own key.

Bone left the kitchen, opened the basement door and called down 'Quinn.'

Nothing stirred. He raised his voice.

'QUINN!'

Upstairs, something abruptly moved.

Bone swung round the newel and was up the narrow flight two at a time. In the pink bedroom, in Claire Fairlie's magnolia-pink sheets, an apparition sat up, shock-headed, staring.

'That's where you got to, is it?' Bone said. 'Out of that, Martin. Up and dressed. You'd no business to come here.'

Martin pushed back the covers. He was naked. Reaching for his clothes, he fell on his knees. Under the bed something, dislodged by his foot, rolled and came to light: a bottle, a whisky bottle, empty. The rest of the room was draped with Claire's clothes, some on hangers, some on chairs, or over the bed-end. A nightdress lay crumpled in the bed. A large pot of bronze chrysanthemums stood on the bedside table, a bronze bow tied round it.

Martin stood up up, trousers in one hand, the other to his head. Bone picked the bottle from the floor and said, 'How much did you have?'

'Don't know. Maybe half.'

'What else have you touched?'

'I don't know. Things.' A hand circled vaguely. 'I ate some biscuits and that.'

Bone said, exasperated, 'You'd better come down.'

'And I used the bathroom.'

'You'd better use it again. A wash may improve the way you feel. Come on, Martin. You've made a proper mess of everything. Treasure let you in, did he?'

'I said I'd sleep on her couch. He told me not to touch anything. I'm sorry. I just—'

He looked ready to cry. Aware how much he would hate that, Bone told him bracingly, 'What's done is done. Come down and you can tell me about it.'

The bathroom held a Christmas cactus in resplendent flower, its voracious brilliant petals spreading over the sill. Talc, hair-colouring spray, nail-varnish, bath-salts filled the ledges. A Kermit was propped, wire arms arranged languorously behind his head, where he could watch her bath. Martin ran water, doused his head, washed generally and personally, and was drying himself on the bath-towel when he saw that Bone was still there in the door.

'Thought you'd gone down. Having a good snoop?'

It was the first snarl. 'I've no interest,' Bone said drily, 'except in the bathroom itself.'

Martin pulled on his clothes.

'Hadn't you a coat? In last night's weather?'

'Teddy said he'd dry it. The boiler's down there.' He swayed. 'I'm still lit.' It puzzled him.

'It takes a while for that much alcohol to get processed. That you haven't thrown up says something for your constitution.'

Martin glanced at the mirror, pushed his hands through his hair to make sure it stood up, and prepared to follow Bone downstairs.

Bone was on the telephone when he arrived, giving the word to the station that he was found. He turned, with what Martin thought was a very uncompromising stare, and pointed to the sofa. Martin sat. Bone rang off and stood, hands clasped behind him, in judicial stance.

'Explain to me: a) why you left your sister alone in the house last night after she'd seen the murdered body of a woman she knew; and b) what you've done in this house—precisely and in detail, up to the moment when you got into bed.'

The last remark was merciful; but Martin had not meant ever to tell about those fantasies in any case.

'Well I just forgot. Prue, I mean. Claire'd been killed. How could I think of anything? Oh God.' His eyes, wide and, it was true, not perfectly focussing, slid away from Bone's regard. 'I don't believe it. I didn't, anyway. I do now. It couldn't happen, though. Even whatever she did, no one could kill her.'

'What did you do at the school, Martin? You arrived for the performance. Go on from there.'

'Well, I sat through it, what else? It was all right. Nice singing, a bit feeble all those girls. The tarts were fun, old Prue really looked something. I was waiting for Claire to show. I went to ask Prue when Claire was due on, but the dragons wouldn't let me through so I nipped out and round the back and asked one of the others, and she said Claire was Mrs Bates or something and she'd be on soon, so I buggered back to my place and the next act had started.'

'Did you see anyone but the girl you spoke to?'

'There was a bloke hanging around in the playground. He was off soon as he saw me.'

'What sort of bloke? Tall? Short?'

'Tallish, but there's not much light except from the windows. Heavy-looking. He went off round the far side, quick like he shouldn't be there.'

'What was he wearing?'

Martin gazed at the nearest plant, unfocussed again, picturing what he had seen. 'Sort of loose short coat, donkey jacket, something like that.'

'And then?'

'Well, I sat through the rest of it. Had to sit in another place not to push past people. Then Mrs Bates never came on. I thought right to the end she would. After all the clapping and everything I went to find Prue and they wouldn't let me in, they said to sit down and wait; dragon with red hair. I waited ages. Then Prue came flying out and said Claire'd been stabbed. Ian Sharpe'd killed her. She looked terrible, Prue was in a state and a half. I didn't believe her, you know, I just thought it was a put-on, but then there was to and fro and I thought, it's true. So I went out.'

'Didn't anyone stop you?'

'Parents of one of Prue's friends were leaving, they had to go home for the baby-sitter, and I went out with them. The teacher on the door wrote their name down. I walked for ages. Up to High Rocks, and then back and round the town. There was this terrific storm and it felt right, I walked through it all. I landed up here. Ted let me in downstairs. He fussed a lot and I let him take my coat to dry and he made me dry my hair and gave me a hot toddy. He was expecting Merc back. I said could I sleep here, on the sofa. He said no, because nothing should be touched. He did say that, it's not his fault I touched things. I told him I wouldn't, I'd just sleep. So after a bit of yes-no he did let me; and I did lie down here and I meant not to touch anything, but I was cold, I thought coffee wouldn't hurt, and there was the whisky, and I thought what the hell.'

He was developing a headache, as his eyes showed. Bone went into the kitchen, got a clean glass and brought him water.

'Drink a lot. Dilute what's left and help the liver.' He turned away, hands in pockets, and paused, looking at the hearth. Martin, dismally drinking, thought there was a stillness about him and looked up. Bone swung to return his gaze and asked, 'Have you been burning something?'

CHAPTER
6

In Break, the wet playground kept the girls in the Hall and
gym. Grue came to tell Charlotte that 'Your father's found my
brother. He's well and safe. I could bash him.'

Mr Hazeley's secretary noticed that his signature was at its
most hieroglyphic that morning. He himself was taciturn and
did not make his usual private call around coffee time. She
decided that it was not a favourable day to remind him about
altering the office space to isolate the noisier office machines
from the staff.

The last lesson before lunch, Four-L had Physics with Miss
Wallace. Ostensibly copying up notes on the last practical,
they were in fact talking, as they had been doing at every
opportunity all morning, about Sugar Plum.

'*Stop* this chatter!' Miss Wallace commanded. Her hands
made little downward gestures like a begging dog off balance.
Beverly Braun, sprawled across her desk and rocking it back
and forth—she had no books on it—muttered, 'Our pet Peke's
in a pet, no error.'

'Miss Wallace, who do you think did it?' asked Caroline
Timmins.

'Really, Caroline, get on with your work. I don't want to
hear a word more on the subject. You know what Miss Mallett
said at Assembly about useless chatter.'

'But what else can we think about?'

'Yes, Wally, murders don't happen every day.'

'I'm not so unfeeling as to talk about it, and neither should you be. Finish your notes.'

'I can't keep my mind on anything, Miss Wallace. I cried all night.'

'Liar,' said Beverly.

'I *did*.'

'We think it's Mr Sharpe. Prue Grant found him there.'

'He shouldn't be in school, should he?'

'Should be in prison. How long d'you think he'll get?'

'Life,' Beverly said. She was writing on the desk. The surface was a laminate supposedly graffiti-proof, but she had a compass point. Miss Wallace suddenly saw this and cried, 'Beverly! Stop that at once!'

Beverly raised her eyes only and stated 'Fuck off.'

There was a short silence, Miss Wallace frozen, as Beverly later said, like a rampant weasel. A girl said, 'You shouldn't let her get away with that, Wally.'

'I won't be spoken to like that, Emma. My name is Miss Wallace and I don't in the least require your advice.'

'All right, all right,' Emma cried, indignant but placatory.

'Don't answer me back. You can have a detention.'

'You can't . . . It's end of term . . . No more detentions . . .' came the general shout. From the back row a soft mutter, resembling footsteps peglegging along a corridor, set up. 'Silly wally, silly-wally, silly-wally silly-wally . . .' They accelerated.

'Sugar Plum was to have taken next detention,' someone said. The girl next to her burst out hysterically crying. Beverly seized her by the shoulder and threatened her with the compass point. 'Shut up, Mairi you berk.'

It was then that it struck Miss Wallace that, apart from and accompanying the distractions, most of the girls were in fact getting on with their work, in a desultory way. Mairi's boo-hooing was too customary to attract much notice, loud though it was.

The door did open, however. Miss Wallace quivered but it was not Miss Mallett or any even more portentous form, only her own senior, Miss Lashmar. The girls rose, even Beverly with a concussed desk juddering at her thighs.

'Sit down, girls. I just looked in,' she added to Miss Wallace, 'to borrow a copy of Jensen.' She bent to rootle in the bench drawer at Miss Wallace's side and murmured genially, 'Isn't it impossible to get them to do any work today?'

Miss Wallace's red bow bobbed in delighted acquiescence. Straightening up, Miss Lashmar said, 'My dear Mairi! Miss Wallace, may I take her out? Come along, Mairi.'

Miss Wallace was left dazed and grateful. Her predicament then, today at least, was general. Miss Lashmar, shepherding Mairi along the corridor, had seen in Miss Wallace's book-bag a luridly coloured travel pamphlet and she was picturing The Wally, bikini'd, on some tropic beach.

Four-L, sensing the relaxation of atmosphere, quarrelled quietly on the length of Mr Sharpe's sentence, congratulated Beverly on Mrs Trapse once more, reminiscing on its glories and, with voices actually hushed, speculated on Miss Fairlie's wounds.

'Prue saw them.'

'She won't talk about it.'

'Sharpie was covered in blood. Dripping.'

'About a dozen yukky—'

'Stop that at once,' said Miss Wallace. They glanced at her, and recognising a genuine tone of voice, stopped. Beverly suddenly rose and sauntered massively to the door.

'Where are you going?' Miss Wallace heard with fury the squeak in her tones. 'Sit down. If you want to be excused . . .'

Beverly did not trouble herself to look or reply, but went out leaving the door to slam. An interested silence fell. Miss Wallace, after a second of gaping at the door, turned round and began cleaning the blackboard.

'Shall I go and see where she is, Wally?'

'Don't be so naïve, she's gone to the bog.'

'Shall I go and tell her to come back?'

'*I'll* go.'

'It's lunchtime anyway.'

'Yes, let us go, ducky Wally. We've finished and it really is all but time.'

'And it's end of term.'

'We *have* to go and see if Sharpie's been arrested yet. It's inhuman to keep us in suspense.'

'Isn't the Superintendent *dreamy*, all blond and pale?'

'That's Cha Bone's father.'

'Everyone knows that. We're hungry, Wally. Be a dear and let us go,' and Alison imitated the bell in a high-pitched buzz. Someone drummed on the desk. Two more began to hum *Why are we waiting?* The noise was considerable but no one came in to object. When the door did open, wide, it was Beverly. She said, 'Anyone for lunch?'

A stampede knocked desks askew; girls crammed the doorway, yelling. Miss Wallace leant on her bench, listening to the din as it retreated down the corridor. It was cut off as by a guillotine. A patter of footsteps, like a sheep herd along a country lane, succeeded. In silence the girls came back, took their places and stood. Miss Mallett, apocalyptic sheepdog, appeared at the door. Miss Wallace rushed to speak.

'The girls thought it was the bell, I think, Miss Mallett.'

A girl flung up a hand and, not waiting, spoke. 'Miss Wallace didn't want us to be late like we were last Wednesday.'

Last Wednesday, a big rehearsal for the Opera, had been the day of the big row because half the school was late for first lunch. The kitchen staff had thrown an epic wobbly. Miss Fairlie had been everywhere, placating, berating, indignant.

'I see.'

She probably did. Headmistresses must regularly announce their omniscience, for disciplinary purposes.

'When the bell goes, leave your seats without talking.'

The bell obediently sounded. The girls obediently filed out. Miss Mallett let them pass her and followed, leaving the door, a duchess unattended by her footman.

Miss Wallace remained frozen for a minute. She felt the rebuke of Miss Mallett's silence. Then, hearing the lunchtime hullabaloo breaking out all over the school, she stepped from her place and scurried smartly around the desks. Some had plain white Formica tops, and these she assiduously read, from *Why won't you talk to me?* to *Giving head is an acquired taste.*

She unlocked her cupboard and extracted her lunch-box. Standing there, she began to snuffle, like a rabbit with a cold.

Ursula Dunne was cleaning up next door, rewinding an audio tape and collecting pictures known as Stimulation Material although they were too mild to approximate even to caffeine, was reflecting guiltily, remorsefully, that it was nice to know her lessons were not going to be interrupted by Claire who, if she was free, used English lessons to take girls out for personal talks.

She heard an odd noise from the Physics lab. She went to look, because it sounded as though Wally was crying. Surely if anyone wouldn't mourn Claire it was Wally, whose disorderly classes were so often walked in on and so easily, scornfully, quietened by her; who so often and so contemptuously had been talked at by Claire in the staffroom.

The red Christmas-present bow bobbed behind the cupboard door. Ursula realised that the noise was Wally laughing.

Soberly she went to lunch.

Bone, catching up on paperwork in the Incident Room at the station, gave Locker a running commentary too.

'He'd searched the whole place, Steve. He couldn't remember what he'd touched or hadn't touched. Must have been smashed as a stoat. And he had burnt letters he'd written to her. Not, he said, and it's possibly true, because he thought they were incriminating but because he was trying to wipe out what he'd felt about her. It occurs to me that he also didn't want them read by the cold eye of the law. Do you remember any schoolboy notes you wrote to girls?'

'Don't think I wrote any love-letters. But equally these might be incriminating?'

'Equally. And if I hadn't found him there, would we have known about them at all? And it's no good giving our Mr Treasure the most almighty rocket although I'm going to, when we ought to have been there all night going through the place.'

'We were both up all night the night before.' Bone had been on duty (break-in on Mount Ephraim) and Locker had a six-month-old child. Bone said, 'No. I know,' and rubbed his neck. He knew whose head would, rightly, roll.

In lunch hour there was a choir rehearsal for the end-of-term carol service; this threw out the usual lunch arrangements and upset the logistics for afternoon games, but the Carol Service now had priority.

There was a division in the choir which had nothing to do with sopranos and altos. Sir Herbert Derwent had written an exquisite acapella arrangement of a recondite carol, which it was now mandatory each year to sing. Each year the tradition was followed by both divisions of the choir.

All of them sang the verse, with what reservations its text might arouse in them:

> *He lieth here*
> *In strawë clear*
> *This babe so fair*
> *He hath no peer*

Then came the chorus, burden or refrain. Julia Craven, and the two prefectly altos who flanked her, sang the correct words; they sang with emphasis because they, but not Sir Herbert, could hear the fourth year altos, and some of the fifth and, dare it be said, the sixth?—singing otherwise.

> *Hear the shepherd's drum*, Julia adjured.
> *Fum, fum, fum*, Tabitha and Janine supplied.

Sweetly came the voices of Kat Hazeley, Prudence Grant, Mairi Leggatt, Zoë Lee and Charlotte Bone:

> *Hear the shepherd's drum—*
> *Bum, bum, bum.*

The tune wound about and the young faces were attentive to Sir Herbert. Fazileh and the sopranos of orthodoxy sang:

> *Hear the shepherd's fiddle,*
> *Do-diddle, do-diddle, do-diddle.*

Emma Jones, Emma Phillips and Caroline Timmins were the clearest in the traditional variant:

> *Hear the shepherd's fiddle:*
> *Po-piddle, po-piddle, po-piddle.*

Herbert Derwent, enraptured by the girls' voices climbing and playing among the harmonies as they all repeated the charming, the rustic refrain, conducted with eyes almost shut, and swayed as his hands delicately conjured. For the girls, the childish subversion offered, this day in particular, a release. It was in fact too much. This day, the carol dissolved in splutters and giggles. Even Julia Craven gasped and blinked against the purging laughter.

Sir Herbert clapped his hands and started the carol again.

Bone walked from his car, past the cinema, down towards Lofting Antiques. The window, when he found it, was crowded. He saw what Treasure had meant by 'junk'; they had not achieved, yet, the chaste connoisseur status of a few very good items of one line on show. This was eclectic: plates, like the decorated ones on the basement stairs of the flat, Kylins ferociously grinning; trivets and trivia; small snuffboxes, one in the shape of a high-heeled eighteenth-century shoe; an Art Deco lamp, the stem a woman in glass draperies. He could see Treasure inside talking to a buyer, one hand caressing the top of a small table they were evidently discussing, the other hand curling expressively in appreciation of the craftsmanship. The buyer crouched to look. There was a negotiation, a chequebook produced.

Bone pushed the door and went in, shut it, began to examine the wares: a patchwork quilt hung on the wall. Cha would love that . . . the price made him take his hand off it. Further back stood a beautiful little harpsichord. Shelves supported more china, leather-bound books of terminal erudition, china boxes with tiny flower sprigs painted in detail, *papier-mâché* boxes lacquered and gilt. Everything was spotless, shining and set out to advantage. The owners had achieved a gloss of success by making everything look valued.

The purchaser went out. Bone turned.

'I think you know,' Bone said with deliberate articulation, 'what I've come to say to you.'

Teddy's fingers flew to his mouth. 'He didn't touch things? Oh no, he didn't? He promised.'

Bone kept silence, a formidable gambit.

'I'm sorry. I shouldn't have, I know I shouldn't. He was so wet, and so miserable, and he promised.'

'Can we talk here?'

Teddy went to the door and turned the notice to 'Closed'. 'It's nearly lunchtime and no one's ever in a panic to buy antiques, are they?' He locked the door and shot the bolts.

He took Bone into the back, a small room with a chintz easy-chair and a tapestry-covered stool, a kettle and tray of china cups, assorted, a small desk with ledgers and a portable type-writer. The foot of a carpeted staircase showed through a door, which Teddy shut. A barred door led to a little yard crammed with a shed, tarpaulin-covered shapes, and two bay trees in white tubs. Teddy saw Bone's idly professional inventory-taking pause at the tubs and said, 'They belong in the front, but we have to take them through at night or they do a disappearing act. We had them *chained* but someone took out the shrubs. Can't always be bothered to lug them through the shop myself. We do have security problems, everyone does, listen to me talking to one who should know. Leonard wants an Alsatian but I can't stand them. Bitten by dogs when I was a little boy and it *traumatised* me. Twice! Used to go on holiday to my Aunt Julie in the country and she had two Highland terriers, nasty little things. Two holidays running they bit me, both of them, in the same place: *on* the landing and *in* the ankle. Proves I have tasty ankles, I suppose. But you won't catch me with a guard dog, not ever. Leonard did have a somewhat reeky little Peke, Choo-choo, but by the end his back legs had gone, paralysed, you know, and he couldn't bark above a wheeze, so bar *saddening* some burglar fatally I don't know what he could have done. If we had an animal I'd prefer a cat. There are mice here. Not so much use as a burglar alarm of course but far more sympathetic. Not any old moggy, I'd like one of character. A cat in a shop lends an aura, softens people, but Leonard's funny about cats the way I am about dogs. I shall get my own way in the end, I always do. Do you know anyone reliable I could get a good cat from?'

Bone did. Thinking of Prue's Colonel Bogus and Posse, he saw himself as fulfilling, whatever his failures as a policeman, a useful role in society as Emily Playfair's agent for the placing of kittens.

'Perhaps. Have you the key for Miss Fairlie's basement door? It's too late but I'd like to have it.'

The repressive tone, and the return to the subject Teddy had tried to talk away, made him serious. He took out his key ring, chained to his belt, and manoeuvred a neat brass key off it.

'I'm sorry. It was stupid of me.'

Bone had intended to say more, but the serious regard met his and changed his mind. 'Yes.'

He sat down in the armchair and said, 'Perhaps you can tell me about Claire Fairlie's visitors and friends.'

'Yes, yes, everything I can. All right if I put the kettle on? I'd best get my lunch now. Well—' he took the kettle to a dark cubby-hole under the stairs, where a dim bulb showed for a moment a lavatory and wash basin. Coming back, he plugged the kettle in and crouched on the tapestry stool. 'Well, we didn't get to see everyone who came, by any means, but Claire would now and then call down to borrow sugar or biscuits. They'd eat her out of house and home. She didn't cook much, and she never baked, so she liked the things I made. You know it is so sad. I'm just coming to know I shan't see her any more. I can't believe there could be a person who'd want to kill her. It must be a madman. But you want to know about visitors. Girls from her school often came, I know. I'm inquisitive, you'll have realised! So I used to peek when I heard her bell.'

Bone, who had been pretty sure of this, went on listening with the more friendly version of his non-committal face, leaning an elbow on his knee.

'It'd be one girl, or two, for a while and then suddenly a different one. She coached them, I believe, and she'd help them with their troubles. Haven't things improved? Catch any of my schoolteachers helping me with my troubles. She was very sincere, really tried, spent hours with them. Sometimes she'd talk about them, but not their names. She'd ask our advice.'

Bone tried to imagine Merc giving advice. Teddy made tea and opened a packet of lunch and a biscuit box. 'Tea, Mr

Bone? Biscuit? I just have this roll for lunch, don't eat much at mid-day. What about your lunch?'

'I'm eating later. Go ahead. Tea will be welcome.'

'She was coaching Martin for A-levels. She'd discuss his set books with Merc. He was at Oxford, you know, at Oriel.'

Bone held his calm with an effort. Merc discussing books was surprise enough, but Oxford? What had he read? And how had he managed a viva?

'Then there was that nice girl Kat. Looked like one too, great green eyes, lovely white skin. Claire was very sweet to her because she was having such trouble at home, getting beaten up, you know. Difficult to believe, isn't it? My own family was always so loving.'

Bone looked at Teddy's face, still slightly chubby under his thinning hair, wistful now for the parents who had hugged him. Did they know he was gay? Had they accepted it or lived in happy ignorance still hoping for his 'settling down', for grandchildren?

'Kat used to come back with Claire from school and she'd give her coffee and baby her a bit. She liked the little cakes I make and they used to come downstairs sometimes and once, I remember, Merc was there and she had these nasty bruises on the tops of her arms all over that white skin. Purple and yellow, like pansies growing in the snow Merc said afterwards. He's such a poet.'

Pansies in the snow! Real *fleurs du mal*. Bone reminded himself it might be true Merc was a poet. He might even, in Bone's absence or the absence of company, be loquacious. It was something you should never forget, that people could show one image to the world quite different from the one that friends see.

'Kat stopped coming after her father came. One night there was this terrific row, the bell ringing, and when Claire answered he was shouting so you could hear every word, "What do you mean, setting my daughter against me, interfering bitch?" and stuff like that. I trembled for Claire, I can tell you. Wished Merc was in. I was nearly going to be brave and go upstairs and get beaten up *with* her, couldn't help thinking of those bruises on Kat, but suddenly all quiet on the Western front, not a murmur. I sat there, bun half-way to my mouth, and listened. Thought maybe he'd struck her dead. Oh Lord.' For a moment he stared at Bone, considering the present alongside the past.

'Well, I did wonder, but no sound, he didn't leave and after a bit there were sounds and voices. He didn't leave, at least not until early morning.'

His eyebrows marked the significance.

'He wasn't the only one that stayed, mind. It was her business and I wasn't that interested. Took it for granted, a girl as pretty as Claire.' He started to cut up an apple and went on thoughtfully, 'I can't recall that Kat came at all after her father did. Suppose he told her not to. It was a shame he hit her, she's a lovely girl.'

'All right to hit the ugly ones?' Bone asked.

'Oh dear. What one says without thinking. It's true it seems worse when a person's good-looking, but it oughtn't, no. I'd said to Claire what about the NSPCC and she said she might as a last resort. But that was before. After that evening I think he came round quite often. He'd arrive late and leave after midnight. Heavy feet, like your Inspector. You're light-footed, I thought it was Claire when I heard you first. So was Ian.'

'Did you meet Fairlie's men friends often?'

'Oh no, I kept myself *to* myself when they were around. She would chat about them, and I knew what they looked like because of my peeking, though I'm not so sure I'd know Michael, Kat's father. I got a real turn over Ian, though. I was coming back late from a party, towards two o'clock. Not much of a party, leaving at that time, but never mind the side issues. I was the other side of the road from our place and just crossing between two parked cars when I saw there was someone in the car in front. He was staring with those big round eyes up at Claire's window. Well, I went across smartish, minding my own business, but no mistaking him. He never saw me, but then he never did see me, if you know what I mean. He'd decided I was a bad smell and told Claire she should get rid of us out of the house. Well, I told *Merc* that morning when he came in and after that he used to look out for Ian's car. Two or three times a week it'd be there.'

Bone remembered Sharpe's rejection of spying on her: *hardly dignified or reasonable*, was it? Undignified and unreasonable, the man had done it.

'Merc said, suffering grinding torments. Ian was always uptight, you know. Merc said he always held himself as if he had a stair rod up his bum—if you'll pardon the phrase.'

Bone registered that the poet in Merc did not always demand lyrical expression.

Treasure had little more to tell him. Bone took his leave, and headed for Marks and Spencer for sandwiches for lunch. He and Cha must do some shopping for the freezer, but he was too hungry to think about it now. He took one of the perennial prawn mayonnaise, and the last egg and cress, and strode off for a working lunch.

The girl in the window had red hair, a bit like Barbara's. It reminded him of what he had almost forgotten. There was a chill wind today and not many people sitting on the benches in Calverley Road, still damp from last night's rain. It was one of his days for feeling tired, though, and he sat there, watching the people who walked up and down the pedestrian precinct, going into shops and coming out. They had told him he would have to keep searching. He couldn't consider his work done. He hated the two women who came out of Marks and Spencer, a little to the right of his bench, carrying bright green plastic bags and talking about him. That started up the group of teenagers standing not far away, one of them rearing up with his bike every now and then, and thudding the front wheel to the ground. When they, too, began to talk about him he had to get up and leave. They never looked at him, which was clever. They could make their voices louder so that he could still hear them as he reached the traffic lights. One day they would all be sorry.

CHAPTER
7

Bone walked up the school's shallow entrance steps and through the handsome double doors. He caught the dying shrill of the bell and instantaneously the hall flooded with girls. Most hurried, some turned to stare, some to nudge and giggle. Miss Wallace, weaving rapidly through, caught sight of him and dropped all her books. The girls treated this obstruction like a stone in a river, swirling either side but not stopping. Bone and a tall Far Eastern girl — was it last night's pianist? She looked so different in uniform — bent to help her pick everything up. He had admired that brilliant piano work last night––was it possible it had been last night? She moved away as he was about to congratulate her.

He handed the retrieved books to Miss Wallace and was startled to see that she looked frightened. Was it habitual? Did life itself terrify her? He had thought he was wearing one of his amiable expressions. She was uttering—had been all along—an undercurrent of apologies and thanks. Now she scurried away. Bone turned to see Mr Sharpe passing; he glanced at Bone as if he wondered why this stranger was in the building, then shut his mouth repressively, either of Bone or of himself, and was gone. He could scarcely have looked more disapproving had Bone been a murderer.

Entering the secretary's room to give polite notice of his arrival, Bone found Miss Mallett installed there. She was wearing, he was delighted to see, a burnous of cream and scarlet.

'Good afternoon, Mr Bone. Much the simplest thing was for your people to take over my room, and Miss Cantrell and I are quite comfortable for a few days here. I understand they have put another telephone in temporarily. Mr Locker is working there.'

Bone said the appropriate grateful things. In comparison with Room Seven, this was handsome.

'Please do not hesitate to tell me of any way in which we can assist the enquiries.'

It is always more pleasant to be told to do your job in a gracious manner. Bone, trained to ask for facilities he needed in any case, was rather charmed by her affability.

Locker, installed behind Miss Mallett's desk, had opened a window. Despite a faint flurry of snow outside, the room had not quite lost its oppressive heat.

Locker got up to give place, but Bone, taking off his mac, sat in the wing-chair and said, 'What have we got, Steve?'

'Motives. A bit vague.' He was doubtful, pulling his under-lip. 'Miss Wallace acted oddly when I talked to her. Bit eccentric not to say weird, but I gather everyone's used to her. She's the one you'd pick to be a typical spinster schoolteacher. When she answered she was strange, gave the impression of suppressing either crying or laughing. She's got a red bow on.'

'Reminded me of those aristocrats during the French Revolution who wore red ribbons round their necks to mock the guillotine.'

'She was certainly relieved at Fairlie's death. "Such a cruel woman", was her song. And it comes out too that Fairlie was angling for Mrs Lambert's job. It was common knowledge she thought Lambert not much good at it, used to get in little criticisms and try to deal with the girls herself; so I took it up with Miss Mallett and she said Fairlie had approached her. She'd temporised, that was her word, thinking Fairlie was not sufficiently impartial, "was good at initiating policies but found it not so easy to pursue them." Here is Mrs Garland, Miss Lashmar, Mrs Shaw all saying Fairlie never let slip a chance of talking against Lambert's competence behind her back. Mrs Garland and the P.E. teacher hear the girls talking among themselves a lot, and the girls said they thought Fairlie would be next Deputy Head, that—' Locker consulted notes— 'Baa-Lamb would get the push. Others said Mrs Lambert wouldn't stand for it and was sick of Fairlie's fishing. Well, it's far-fetched as a motive for murder, but we've seen funnier ones.'

'We don't know what went on behind scenes. Constant dropping weareth away stone, and I wouldn't say I've never had a colleague I wanted to bop over the head.'

Bone got up and, almost out of habit, made a tour of Miss Mallett's bookshelves. One held a Greek lexicon and Latin texts, beside a row of books on comparative religion, the Koran, the Bible, *In Search of the Miraculous*, Tagore, *Buddhism and Western Man*. He moved on to the shelf near her desk: volumes of Harold Nicolson; *A Room of One's Own; A Time of Gifts*; Wainwright's *Fell Walking*, at which Bone suffered a brief crippling vision of Miss Mallett, booted, striding up Scafell; Boswell's *Johnson* and, more unusually, Dr Johnson's actual Dictionary along with other dictionaries and a Thesaurus.

Locker said, 'Kh'h'hm,' and Bone became aware of patience behind him, the unsaid *Is Miss Mallett a suspect?*

Bone shed his jacket as well and sat, clasping his hands before him, and gave Locker a smile.

He smiled rarely and did not know the effect it had in a face that tended to bleakness. His common social smiles, being tight-lipped, were not encouraging. Locker expanded. 'Here's the list I've been compiling.' He brought it across. 'Here's the names of all those in the vicinity at the relevant time, here's details against the names.'

Girls playing Ladies of the Town, and a list of names. 'Macheath': Sarah Crouch, 'Filch': Anne Higgins, Prompt: Samantha MacGregor, Prefect: Fazileh Rashidi. Miss Wallace, Mrs Lambert, Mr Sharpe. Man peeping, Harry Birch.

Bone's pen added a name. He handed the list back.

'Martin Grant? I passed your message that he was found, to his sister. He was there?'

'He told me so with his own pearly lips. Found him in Claire Fairlie's bed this morning.'

Locker's eyes gratifyingly took on the size of the Round Tower of Copenhagen. 'In her bed? I locked that basement door. You saw me do it. Had he her key?'

'No. Our Mr Treasure's kind heart and duplicate key opened all to him. Young Martin, in shock we suppose, had been roaming the stormy streets and had come, wet as any drowned rat, to look his last on all things lovely.'

The floweriness of the statement betrayed to Locker that Bone was considerably annoyed. 'Why on earth would he do that, sir? A bit silly, if he'd thought what the circumstances are.'

'We've both been seventeen, Steve. It's a disease, rarely fatal, in which doing silly things is one of the persistent symptoms.'

'They don't live in the real world.' Locker felt comfortably certain that he did.

'What's that when it's at home? We have to keep in mind that murderers don't live in the real world either. Whether they build up to it or break into it suddenly, they're acting from a cockeyed viewpoint in which nothing, nothing at all, is as important as their own immediate need. They see this human life as worth less than their own need, their need for revenge or peace of mind or pride. Martin Grant may be silly. He may be rather smart. He's managed to touch most of the things in that house and also to burn his letters to Fairlie.'

'Had he written the one we found?'

'Oh yes. He didn't appear to mind its being found. His act, if it is one, is the rejected boy who wanted to get rid of all that was to do with his dead, in every sense, love.'

Locker chewed the end of his biro. 'Is he on anything?'

'He says not. He'd been drinking.'

'Rumours here that some of the girls do drug.'

'Of course. Whether they do or not, some of them are bound to have said they do. And this school, for all its ladylike appearance and genuine good standards, has its share of tearaways.'

Something thudded against the study door and, though muffled by its august thickness, young female voices skirled. Locker moved with his usual surprising speed, opened the door with the traditional 'Now then,' and was almost winded by two struggling girls, each with one arm in the grip of W.P.C. Fredricks.

'I was *sent* for.'

'I've *got* to see them *now*.'

Bone watched Locker, merely by moving, get them both outside. In a moment he reappeared, ushering a wild-haired girl, hollow eyed, a cinch for an inhabitant of the blasted heath if she were not also young and very pretty.

She came forward while Locker went to request Miss Mallett's presence, and she stood twisting her fingers and hands together. Miss Mallett took the chair by the closed window's radiator.

'Can we start with your name?' Bone asked, while Locker's pen hovered over the list of those whose parents had given permission for interview.

'Mairi Leggatt. I was meant to sing Mrs Trapse yesterday.' Her eyes, slightly bloodshot and definitely red-rimmed, hovered, shifted and failed to fix on anything. There was a pause.

'I saw your name on the programme,' Bone said. 'You didn't sing, though.'

'She made me ill, you see. Poisoned me. I couldn't sleep, and couldn't sleep, and awful nightmares. Stage fright, honestly, that was crap.'

Miss Mallett, whose instinct must surely be to restrain such language on her pupils' lips, did not stir.

'Who had stage fright?'

'Me, but I didn't. The doctor said, stupid old berk. Mummy got the doctor this morning.'

'I see.'

Locker's eyebrows plaintively told that he didn't. Bone elucidated. 'You were so ill this morning, after not sleeping and then having awful nightmares, that your mother called the doctor.'

'Took me to the surgery. Lot of use that was. No use at all. I mean is there any use in me telling the old stick-in-the-mud that never listens anyway?'

This coherent sentence heartened Bone. He said, 'Try me. I'm listening.'

Her eyes went past him and fixed on the Cranach print over the bookshelves.

'Mairi. What could you have told the doctor?'

'About the poison.'

'You were poisoned?'

'Yes I was. I really was. I bloody—' and abruptly conscious of Miss Mallett, she fell silent. Bone got up, went round the desk and bent to pencil on Locker's notepad *High?*

Locker ticked it.

'You're still not well, are you, Mairi?'

'I'm all right. Old Doctor Family Doctor Fool said so. Only nerves, stage fright, panic.' Her eyes shifted. She said, 'Panic danceth before him, his neesings flash forth light,' and looked, puzzled, at Miss Mallett.

'It might be best for you to go home, Mairi, and sleep until you feel better, and then you can tell Mr Bone all about it.'

'I can't go home. Mummy's out.'

'You may lie down in sick-bay, Mairi.'

Mairi clasped her head. 'Oh *shit!*' she cried out. 'I can't get it to go straight. Like dreams. Listen. Beverly poisoned me with Smarties to get her part back. I'm not swearing, Miss Mallett. They're right, you have to get your head straight.'

'When you are better, you can tell us what you want to say.'

'But important. If you listen I can tell you now. You think you know it all, stand there like pillows. Oh please listen.'

'What Smarties did Beverly give you?'

'No, not at all. She said and I thought they were. Smarties are good. These had a name on. Writing on them.'

'They were in fact pills?'

'Pills. Make me feel marvellous, see? The difficult bits would be easy. *Bill like a dove,*' and she broke out incongruously in an alto too deep for a skinny body, up and down two notes. 'You can't always get it if you're tense. Sugar coached me. Gave me the part so as not to waste my voice because I'm leaving, but Bev did mind even if Sugar, Miss Fairlie, said she didn't. If she didn't mind why did she poison me? Bev does what she likes. You see? Bev poisoned me so she could have her part back and then Sugar barged in and took it so she's dead, you see?'

'You've said what you wanted to say,' Bone conceded. 'Thank you. And now . . .' He turned towards Miss Mallett, who came forward.

'And now you shall sit with Miss Cantrell until someone can see you to sick-bay, where you can rest. You have told the Superintendent what was on your mind, so you can rest now.'

She put a hand towards Mairi's shoulder, but the girl slid her own hand into it like a child's, and let herself be led to the secretary's office.

Bone and Locker waited for Miss Mallett to reappear. The calm front she had shown to Mairi was gone when she came back. 'This is very disturbing. We've recently been discussing the possibility that some of the girls may be experimenting with drugs, and have been keeping our eyes open, but how could Mairi be in that condition without anyone noticing? And the accusation against Beverly Braun!'

'Which cannot be taken as any kind of evidence, Miss Mallett. There's the possibility, you understand, that it was given while under the influence of some kind of drug.'

Miss Mallett drew breath. Her head went back. 'Is it something for which you will have to arrest her?'

'It's not a crime, Miss Mallett. Unless she decides to drive a car. Her parents could get tests to show what she's taken, perhaps. It may still be traceable. She seems to have taken it of her own free will, though.'

'I should like to speak to Miss Cantrell.' Miss Mallett picked up the telephone and moved a lever on the base of it and pressed a button. Bone had not seen an instrument like that since his childhood, in his uncle's office. 'Miss Cantrell, please don't say any names if the girl is still there. I should like you to try her home number until you get hold of the parent, or try any other number we have on her card; ask the parent to come and collect her. She should be at home.'

The receiver squawked acquiescence.

'Thank you.' Replacing it, Miss Mallett said, 'Perhaps you should speak to Mrs Shaw. She gives very good talks to her classes about drugs, and I believe has read a great deal on the subject.'

'Have you had the police lecturer talk to the school?'

'A young uniformed officer did come,' Miss Mallett said, her tone altering subtly. 'He was kind enough to instruct the girls how to sniff glue.'

Locker exclaimed. Bone recollected complaints he had come

across about a young sergeant zealously lecturing in schools about the dangers of kidnap and rape. This sounded like more of the same.

'Indeed, yes. He explained about the plastic bag, the dollops of glue, the way to hold it. He added that it caused sores, moronic behaviour and frequent brain damage, but he did not seem at all aware that curiosity and experiment are far more vital in children's lives than probable results. Mrs Shaw did say that she did much remedial work based on that talk, so it was useful.'

'I think we might talk to Mrs Shaw.'

They saw the girl who had been waiting, a routine interview, and the bell then rang for next lesson. Miss Mallett went to sit with Mrs Shaw's form. 'They are unlikely, being second years, to be engaged in vital work this week.'

So Mrs Shaw arrived.

She was a slender woman, not tall, with cropped blonde hair. She wore a loose indigo and green check shirt belted on the hips, over blue trousers. She met their regard with astonishing green-grey cats' eyes. 'Into the hothouse. What can I do for you gentlemen?'

The words, Scots and soft-spoken, went with a dancing look. Bone thought that the small pupils that made her eyes so surprising almost suggested she herself was 'on something'— and he was so startled to find the idea violently repellent that he did not speak. Locker, therefore, began the subject. Bone even missed what he said, but watched her sit in the wing-chair, relaxed, her legs out before her with ankles crossed, elbows on the chair arms and thin fingers laced across her chest.

'Knowledge about drugs is part of the syllabus. It used to be a peripheral topic in the fifth year, but now even here in a country town we start lower down the school. As to the other part of the question, I can't say with any certainty how much experimenting there is.'

Bone moved to lean on the desk. Locker waited a moment for him to speak, then asked, 'What do you teach about the subject?'

She gave Bone a glance, as if she thought he had spoken, but answered Locker. 'The varieties of the common drugs that can be abused, and their results, physical and social. Or in fact anti-social. It amounts to a basic briefing, to quote the title of one of the source-books. It's a dodgy subject, you'll understand. You can excite an interest rather than convey a warning.'

'Don't they listen to the warnings?'

'For a good many adolescents, the picture of going to the bad is spectacularly dramatic. You could look at it this way: if cigarette smoking were the habit exclusively of squalid old people and middle-class pundits, we'd not get half the young ones at it. There *was* one class who declared they were thoroughly put off it by a film of an old man in a hospital bed, dying of emphysema and sucking away at a cigarette with pathetic greed. But drugs are glamour.'

Bone listened. It was one of his private nightmares. Charlotte, motherless, handicapped, looking for compensation, for a release, for something. It did not chime with his daytime knowledge of Charlotte, but his profession had given him unwelcome knowledge of another kind: parents, amazed, angry, declaring to him, 'My daughter would never ... I know her, I'm her father—her mother—and I tell you it's impossible.' They could be tearful, they could be furious, but almost all were patently sincere. They knew their child. This child was incapable of theft, arson, drug taking, whatever it had, in fact and patently, done.

'What about the adverts, the ones that concentrated on the squalor and the sickness?' he suggested.

She sat up and leant forward, turning the brilliant eyes on him. 'There's an age when ruining your life has a weird magnificence about it. That prospect is not half the deterrent it is to us. It is growing old that fills them with dismay. Middle age is hard to sell to the young. They'd rather burn out at twenty-one or kick it in the head when they're twenty-five. And decadence has a terrible appeal.'

'If evil had no appeal I'd be out of half my job,' he said. The green in her jersey seemed to be reflected in her eyes. 'But do you think, as an opinion merely, that anyone in the school is experimenting with, or using, any drugs?'

'Mairi Leggatt certainly took an amphetamine yesterday. She says Beverly gave it to her. Beverly Braun. They're not so easy to get hold of nowadays, and Mairi reacts to them badly.'

Locker said, 'We've got no permission to talk to the Braun girl.'

'I talked to her,' Mrs Shaw said. 'She denies it, but then,' with a sardonic tilt of the head, 'she would, wouldn't she? It's likely she did. I dare say she expected to be given her part back if Mairi couldn't do it. A year ago when we were discussing pills she said her mother used uppers because of the long hours she worked. She's a hairdresser, running her own business and her hours can be from nine till seven, standing. No doubt that's why you've not been able to get her to come along, or even answer the telephone.'

'And the father?'

'I'm not sure but that he's a Civil Servant who followed his job to Tyneside or such parts and Mrs Braun with her hairdressing business couldn't go along. There may be other reasons. The girl's not in my form, but as she is something of a problem we all know a bit about her.'

'Does she take your subject?'

'Yes, and she's interested and bright.'

'What about her temperament?'

'She can be subversive and, I've heard, rude.'

'Do you think she would bear grudges, for instance?'

'I've not come across vindictiveness. I'd say she has influence among her set, and a strong sense of justice.'

Bone supposed that Charlotte might constitute a problem too. One that was discussed at staff meetings. His own circumstances were therefore commonly known. This intelligent, alert woman might have heard of Petra's death, of the smash that crippled Charlotte and killed the baby. Used to a personal anonymity when he was working, he felt the awkwardness of it. Embarrassment to Charlotte of having him at work in the school had occurred to him; the reverse had not. Nothing in Miss Mallett's bearing had so far conveyed to him that he was not merely Detective-Superintendent Bone but also Charlotte's father.

Subliminally, as usual, the jarring memory of the smash visited him and was gone. He sighed sharply, left the desk and sat on one of the moquette chairs. He said, 'What about the staff's attitude to Miss Fairlie?'

Locker shifted. Mrs Shaw gave him a direct unsurprised regard.

'The predictable reply is the actual one. Some thought her an admirable woman, an excellent teacher for whom nothing was too much trouble, a possible Deputy Head, and some thought her cruel.'

'Cruel?'

'As an instance, Beverly Braun. As a Problem, she got a deal of attention and help from Claire Fairlie. She was encouraged in her acting and singing, and Claire prevailed on Sir Herbert to give her a part in the Opera when he'd booted her out of Music for misbehaving. Beverly responded very well. Then suddenly Mairi Leggatt was the lame duck, or lame dog. Sir Herbert, who very decently had let Bev try for Mrs Trapse, and had worked with her, found he was landed with Mairi, with a voice of course far better but no acting ability. By this time, Claire wasn't doing much rehearsing either, because of exam coaching, so Ursula Dunne coped. I thought Bev took the demotion pretty well. Claire of course talked to her, presenting Mairi's case, that she's leaving, has a lovely voice, should have the chance and so forth. She told us Bev said she didn't care, and at the time it struck me Claire wanted to take that at face value.'

'And you thought it wasn't true.'

'I thought it far more likely was a defensive retreat, a declaration that she was not going to admit she was hurt. I don't know. What I did think outrageous was Claire's taking the part herself when Mairi fell ill, and when she knew Beverly could have done it. I didn't say anything. One doesn't. It was—an aggrandisement. An ego trip. She could seem to be stepping into the breach at short notice so bravely . . . and nobody said anything.'

She contemplated this for a moment.

'There wasn't much time to say anything, which seems of importance now. Yesterday was unreal because of the performance in the evening. Various flaps taking place, everyone excited. Some of us fairly detached because it wasn't our pigeon. I helped in the dressing and make-up of the principal singers but once they'd gone down I was an usher and then sat in the audience. When Bev came on as Mrs Trapse I was very pleased, pleased Claire had had second thoughts.

'Which, you know, she might have done. She might very well have done. She was impulsive and I suppose her cruelties were—were inadvertent. She'd take up a new cause, a new person, with all her heart.'

'That gives me a good picture of her. Thank you. What about enemies, however? Whom could she have hurt to such an extent that they killed her?'

Mrs Shaw thought. Bone reached for, and turned round, the list of staff names. Grizel Shaw. It was astoundingly inappropriate.

'No.' She raised her head. 'She'd upset a few people, but I don't believe the ones I know of are capable of that.'

Bone pursued gently. 'Who are they, Mrs Shaw?'

'Why, Beverly for one. Mairi is convinced of it.' She smiled; a wide and brilliant smile. Bone found he had smiled too.

Locker made his 'Kh'h'm,' and Bone half-turned his hand, in invitation or permission, and Locker said, 'Hadn't she hurt Mr Sharpe?'

'There were rumours about that,' she said. After a moment both men realised that she did not intend to say more.

'But you don't know any more?' Locker hinted.

'I don't know enough to form an opinion.'

The bell went. She said, 'I have a sixth year class now. Do you want—?'

Bone rose. 'No. No, at present. Nothing else.'

She must go.

CHAPTER
8

It came to Bone that Cha, achieving the top marks of her year
in Biology last July, had told him that Mrs Shaw was the nicest
teacher of all. The remark, which hadn't meant much before,
now meant this vivid woman. He would have met her if he had
not missed the Parent/Teachers' meeting earlier in the term.
Speculation on the reasons why dressing like a boy made a
woman look more feminine was interrupted by Locker, before
him, pointing at a list.

'B. Braun's mother rang at lunchtime saying she'd gone
home and she was keeping her home because she was so upset.'

'Mairi Leggatt might say it was from another cause.'

'About the pills and trying to poison her?'

'M'm. My picture of Beverly Braun is not one of a girl likely
to be upset, or afraid of anything much.'

'Bit of a character, she sounds.'

'I once had a superior who loved American gangster movies
but would not descend to speaking their language. He would
call the Braun girl not "a tough cookie" but "a durable biscuit".'
Bone discovered that Charlotte's being top in Biology was a
delightful thing. He caught Locker's eye surveying him, and
became very businesslike.

'From seeing Miss Braun at last night's performance I'd say
that to ring in with the news she was upset is rather like the
QEII staying in harbour because it was feeling a bit faint.
We'll ring her mother and ask to see her at home. Where is the
shop?'

'Rowan Way; and they live with *her* mother, a Mrs Staice, in St Aubyn Road.'

'You've done your homework, Locker, B plus. And as the mother's hard to get hold of I'll call at the shop, or salon or—'

Men's voices shouting in the hall made a noise strange and barbaric in a girls' school. Bone and Locker strode to the door. Pinned against one of the gold-lettered notice-boards, Mr Sharpe was being shaken by a larger, blond-red man, who had him by the lapels and was slamming him against the oak to punctuate his tirade. Sharpe's part in the dialogue was 'Stop, stop, stop.' His glasses were coming off. The bigger man, hunch-shouldered in a dark grey business suit, was comparing him to various inferior life-forms. Locker reached them and, as the big man paid him no attention but bawled 'Murderer' down into Sharpe's owl-like face, he took him by the upper arms from behind in a grip that made his hands spring open and his head go back. Released, he whirled on Locker with a macerating blue glare. 'Who the hell are you?'

Doors were open by now, all round. Miss Mallett approached. Bone said, 'We're police. Who are you, sir?'

Mr Sharpe's books were scattered like a pool on the floor. The big man's foot was on one of them. Pulling his sleeves and jacket down, the big man said, 'Police, are you? Then why the hell don't you arrest this—' and his hand thrust Sharpe against the wall once more. 'He's your murderer. Why ponce around looking for anyone else?'

'Please come this way, Mr—'

'Hazeley. Michael Hazeley.' He made no move to accept Bone's invitation, so Bone took the other course and walked off disregarding him. He wanted very much to talk to Hazeley and, as he had expected, Hazeley followed him. They left Sharpe to Miss Mallett.

'I've been out all day and on return I find the school has rung asking my permission for you to interrogate my daughter, and that they then rang again to cancel the request because they'd received permission from no less a person than my wife.'

'Well, Mr Hazeley?'

'Well? It's not well at all, let me tell you. My wife left her home eighteen months ago, a fact of which the school is well aware, and she has no rights in the matter. I refuse permission. I'll not have my daughter bullied by police.'

Bone firmly repressed *prefer to do it yourself, do you?* and said, 'Miss Mallett was present during all interviews. Inspector Locker spoke to Katherine this morning. She wasn't able to tell us anything of moment. You've made a note, Mr Locker, that Katherine Hazeley is not to be asked anything more?'

'Yes, sir.'

'Won't you sit down, Mr Hazeley?'

'Why should I?' The hot blue eyes looked Bone over. 'I've told you my considered opinion of who's the murderer.'

'Law courts have this fiddly insistence on evidence,' Bone said. 'As you were acquainted with Miss Fairlie, perhaps you can tell us actual facts on which to base a case.'

'"Acquainted" with Miss Fairlie? What in your nasty little police minds do you mean by that?' His face now wore a smile of pure aggression. 'Interrogating my daughter gave you the news, I suppose.'

'No. We had other sources.'

'The little queen downstairs, was it? What an unsavoury job yours is.'

'Thank you, sir.' Bone blandly took the remark as sympathy, and saw the shift in Hazeley's expression. 'When did your acquaintanceship with Miss Fairlie begin?'

'I met her at parent-teacher bunfights.'

'When did you first visit her at home?'

'A few weeks ago, I suppose. I don't keep a diary of my personal life.'

'"A few weeks" might bring us to November? October?'

'I've no idea.'

'Before your daughter's half-term?'

'What's it matter? I don't know when her damned half-term was. There's a murderer walking round her school and you're busy with prurient little enquiries about my private life.'

'Why should Mr Sharpe have done it?'

'Because the little worm's besotted with her and she gave him the push. She turned him down. By God, he was found with the body, wasn't he?'

'Very likely in the Middle Ages that would have been accepted as proof,' Bone said off-handedly. 'Perhaps if you try to
connect the start of your acquaintance with Miss Fairlie to
some business date, you may be able to place it more exactly.'

Hazeley consented to think about it, but with impatience.
'Oh, say October.'

'What reason had you for calling on Miss Fairlie at home?'

'I thought she was interfering between my daughter and me.
Setting Kat against me. I was wrong,' he added, with a faint
grandeur about the admission that underlined its handsomeness.

'You saw her again after that?'

'It's no secret. We've dined out together.'

'You visited her at home frequently?'

'From time to time. Can't say how often. No idea.'

'An estimate. Once a week, twice a week?'

'Suppose you tell me what purpose this dirty-minded prying
has, if any.'

'Suppose you tell me yourself what terms you were on.'

'I had her. That what you want? And yes, quite often. Spent
evenings there at least once a week, perhaps three nights
sometimes. It was an affaire.'

'And the last such evening?'

'About ten days ago. On the third.'

'Quite a gap.'

'Hardly your business, is it?' He shot his cuffs and smoothed
down his tie, a pink slub silk.

'You gave the impression that you were seeing her more
often than that.'

'Are you—' with that sudden fierce smile—'trying by any
chance to trap me in some way?'

Bone in his turn gave a very brief meaningless grin. If
Hazeley saw that a cooling affaire might be reason for murder,
he was right to be cautious. Sharpe had said she was being
more kind to him lately. Perhaps she had been finding Hazeley
more than a bit savage, perhaps hard to control?

'You last visited her house on the third, you said. Did you
meet her anywhere else since then?'

'No.'

'Talked on the phone?'

'No.' Abrupt and annoyed this time. Had she rung off on him?

'Were you here for the performance last night?'

'No. Amateur opera. No thanks. I had dinner with friends. Pearsall the lawyer and his wife, as I suppose you will ask.'

Bone nodded politely. The Pearsalls lived across the Common, at no great distance. 'At what time?'

'Getting on for eight. I'd a phone call from New York that kept me or I'd have been there nearer seven thirty. I was there until after midnight.'

'Was your call from New York dialled or through operator?'

'An operator.'

'Thank you, Mr Hazeley.'

'Free to go? Brilliant.'

Without another look he stalked out.

'First check the phone call and Sam Pearsall, Steve.'

'I should think she did herself a bit of good seeing less of that one,' Locker said. 'He could have done the stabbing, but it doesn't seem he could have been here.'

'I don't see him as a man who'd stab in the back. Psychological judgements are dicy things and that's off the cuff, but don't you think he'd prefer to see what he was doing? Watch the effect for his own satisfaction?'

The phone rang. Bone took the call. The post-mortem report had arrived at the station. 'Should we send it round, sir?'

'No, keep it. I'll be there; just the main details.'

Sergeant Easton read it out. Bone thanked him and relayed to Locker what they already knew: a puncture wound had hit the shoulder-blade and then a second, luckier or unluckier depending on your point of view, got between shoulder-blade, ribs and spine to penetrate the heart. Death was hastened by removal of the blade and had occurred within seconds. Some force had been necessary to penetrate the musculature and to withdraw the blade afterwards.

'Some force. Well, almost anyone's capable of some force when they're under stress. I'll have to ask Foster about that. I think I'll be off after this Miss Braun. What about you, Steve?'

'I've still paperwork.'

'More remarkable if you hadn't. I'll be there later.'

They put their coats on. Bone looked into the secretary's room to say they were going and to ask Miss Mallett if she would be using her room now. She said she would, so he closed the curtains and switched on the electric fire in the hearth and the room heater.

She came in, saw what he was doing, and thanked him. 'It's very thoughtful of you.'

'It's very good of you to lend us this room.' He made sure nothing of theirs was on the desk; it wasn't. Locker had seen to that. 'I hope there aren't unfortunate consequences to the school from what has happened.'

'A prospective parent has cancelled her appointment. Perhaps it may seem that there is a very bad state of affairs here that something so terrible can occur. An outsider has no way to know how extraordinary, how totally unexpected and unlikely it is.'

Bone kept to himself the speculation that parents might think murder was something infectious, like measles. For one thing, sometimes it was indeed just that, one murder spawned another, a killer felt unsafe, it wasn't so dreadful an act the second time. He was sure Shakespeare said so, probably in *Macbeth*. He was taking his leave when the bell rang.

There had been a certain to-and-fro already, but now doors burst open and shrill voices skirled above the trample of feet. Bone forged out into a *Walpurgisnacht* of squealing, hurrying, barging girls, all laden with vast bags, shouting 'Goodbye' in each other's faces, screeching 'Goodbye' across the lobby at someone going out, fervently embracing friends not seen since forty minutes ago; dodging, running, with some staff flotsam on this uncontrollable flood. Mr Sharpe stood against the honours board as though Hazeley had impaled him there fifteen minutes ago. Surely he could not have been there when Hazeley left just now—could Hazeley have resisted another bout of DIY on the wall? Sharpe detached himself, however, and came towards Bone. At the same moment Bone saw Charlotte making her way. It pleased him that she was able to hold her own in this crowd. Once she came near she hesitated. To rush up to him might not be suitable, might be conspicuous, improper in his duty hours. He smiled at her and she halted before them. Sharpe, about to address Bone, said to her dismissively, 'Not now, Charlotte, I'm busy.' Cha's eyes opened wide and then, her face alight with amusement, she turned away. Bone, rather touched by the innocent egotism of Sharpe, bent his head courteously to hear him in the uproar. Sharpe, making displacement gestures with his bow tie and lapels, still showing signs of crumpling after his hammering, was embarrassed. His eyes watched the girls or focussed on Bone's chin or shoulder as he spoke.

'I hope you see how it is, Superintendent. That man is an animal.'

'How are you, Mr Sharpe? Recovered, I hope.'

'An animal.'

A sudden flash of intensity behind the glasses made Bone think that, despite feeble physique, Sharpe might not have come out worst if the struggle had gone on. A rat, half pulped, that with bitter tenacity might twist and give his adversary the final, fatal bite.

'I have not spoken about him until now but you can see for yourself what he is like. She was too kind in putting up with him. She would help anyone with a problem.'

What, Bone thought, was yours?

'I was surprised to see him walk out free.'

'You have witnesses to an assault, if you want to pursue that yourself, sir. If you think there are bruises, a doctor should see them at once.'

'Sue him, you mean? For "assault and battery"?'

'I didn't see him use his fist. I saw only what might be an assault.'

'Ah. Battery, to be sure, would require a blow. I see the etymology. Perhaps I should sue him. The man's psychotic. A menace to everyone. His accusation of me was typical. I'm sure, however, that he will be behind bars for exactly that before I could pursue him in the civil courts.'

Sharpe was off, prodding a girl out of his way.

Charlotte by the door, leaning on the wall as the last girls went out, stood upright smiling. He touched her arm.

'All right?'

She nodded. 'Going to Grue's, stay for homework, back later.'

Mr Grant or Martin would see her home. Although he saw Martin in light rather murkier than before, Bone had no hesitation in trusting Charlotte to his escort. He bent to kiss her goodbye. Then he turned up his collar and plunged into the lamplit dusk.

A TV shop was playing obstreperous carols. Since the power of God was infinite, perhaps He could rest the merry gentlemen in the presence of such a racket, but Bone felt that dismay was a more likely reaction. As the sound died behind him, he remembered Charlotte's ditty and drove under the neon holly chanting to himself.

> *Hear the shepherd's fiddle,*
> *Po-piddle, po-piddle.*

Finding a parking slot at the end of Rowan Way, he walked thronged pavements. A scarlet, scalloped pelmet proclaimed Ladye Fayre. More y's than wise, for sure. To the best of his knowledge the Middle Ages had not been afflicted with that spelling at all. The shop's bow-windows had frosting sprayed on, and a lantern in the centre of each. He stood aside for an emerging client. Before seeing her face, he guessed her generation by the rigid hair-do, baked like a meringue on her head and lightly wrapped in a white transparent scarf. She was shiny and flushed from the dryer.

A draught blew his own hair into his eyes as he pushed the door and entered the scented heat. The lino, the gowns, the hoods of the dryers were scarlet. A row of women sat trapped, their heads prey to gigantic beetles, and a girl called out 'Mrs Farley's finished.' He almost expected one of them to crash fainting from under her hood, but corralled his imagination. A voice replied, 'I'll take her out'—a gangster phrase.

The receptionist continued to file her nails as he stood before the desk. A thin woman with a blow-dryer said 'Candy!' and the girl started and raised her head. The blasé eyelids lifted, she put down the nailfile and wriggled as she reached for the appointments book. Bone was unmoved by this demonstration that he was still fanciable. She said brightly, 'Who's doing you?' and after a faint pause he registered the place as unisex. Indeed, a man was having his hair styled at the mirrors.

'No, I called to see Mrs Braun.'

The girl called 'Brenda!' and the thin woman with the blow-dryer waved a hand, studying Bone in the glass now and then.

'She's just finishing. Won't be a moment.'

He did not wish to identify himself and cause scandal in the salon. The woman was now showing the customer the back of his head. What would happen if someone gave one look and yelled 'Put it all back!'?

Mrs Braun, gaunt as though she smoked instead of eating, very bronzed from a recent and probably Mediterranean holiday, or perhaps from a sunlamp, wore a navy silk shirt and creased blond trousers not very clean. She was hung with gold chains, most of them real gold, on chest and wrists. Her hair had no style at all though it shone with highlights, her brown waves were caught back in a gold clip, like a little girl's. Her eyes, no little girl's, hazel in deep sockets, were knowledgeable and hard. She greeted him with, 'What's the damage, then? Police, aren't you?'

He wondered, as he showed his card, what the ineluctable stamp upon him was.

'This business at Bev's school?'

Bone explained that they had not been able to see Beverly as they had been unable to contact Mrs Braun, and that as she had been kept at home this afternoon—

'The monkey!' said Mrs Braun. She had a cigarette and lighter at the ready, and stopped in appreciation. 'Bleeding monkey. Bunked off, she has, and phoned in. She can do my voice to a T. She's up to all the tricks in the book, Super. She's bright, you know. Not at school maybe, they don't know how to teach her there, can't get her interested half the time and I don't call that good teaching. Expensive, too. But out of class she's bloody quick. If you want someone that notices things, Bev's the one. *Cheryl*! Candy, go and get Cheryl out of the Ladies.'

As the receptionist went, Brenda Braun said, '*And* she's been there twenty minutes. Bit of work will do that one no harm. Trained in London and gets huffed when she can't tell my clients what to do with their hair. Crimping and gel look super on the kids but she's got to take her turn with the old girls too. Just want a word with her before I come along, okay?'

Returning from a brief colloquy with Cheryl, she shrugged herself into a very good fur coat and came with Bone.

'I mostly walk. Need to, after all day in that atmosphere. You'd think I'd be enough on my feet but it's not the same.' She filled Bone's car with scent, cigarette-smoke and a chemical, hair-dye smell. She flipped the ash-tray out at once with a nicotined hand on which the rings slid sideways.

'St Aubyn's Road, isn't it?' he asked, and she echoed his words to Locker, 'Done your homework.'

Beverly must inherit her size from the father who had not yet been mentioned. Mrs Braun waved the smoke away from Bone's face and talked.

'Of course it's a tragedy, a pretty young woman and all that, but believe me she'll have asked for it. Oh she was a cat, was that Claire Fairlie. Treated Bev rottenly, picked her out, made a lot of her, and I don't and won't deny she helped her either, credit where credit's due. But then she dropped her, took up some other girl. She was the kind that flirts with everyone, man woman or dog, know what I mean? Not that I think she was *that* way, Bev would have known. No, she just had to get people to like her. And good at it, she had charm, and she'd take trouble so long as she was interested. Found her out in the end, though. Boyfriend, I bet. Bev says the German teacher was after her and he's a nasty character if you like. Christ, the report he wrote Bev last term. Give it up, I said to her, I'm not having you taught by anyone that can write about you like that. Sue him for libel, I could.'

She crushed the cigarette savagely and got out another. 'I shouldn't say it of anyone but that Sugar Plum got what was coming to her. I mean, God, if we all got what was coming to us we'd none of us be in a good way, right? But I bet she led him on and wouldn't play. He's a nasty bit of work, is Sharpe. If he thought a *man* would come and tell him off at the parents' evening he'd have minded what he wrote about Bev, but he knows her father never comes. Doesn't want to meet me there and that's for sure.' She settled in her seat. 'Told him when I threw him out, I can bring her up on my own, I said, I don't need your help, I don't need a thing from you from now on. And I've kept my word. Well rid of him, gormless shit.' She snorted smoke at the windscreen, and once more wafted it away from Bone. 'Without him to spend my money I can give Bev a better chance.'

At what? Bone thought. His present impression was that if Beverly had learnt the sort of lesson her mother was teaching, she might well have knifed Claire Fairlie: and if she had, her mother would most probably admire her spirit and blame Fairlie alone.

'Here at the end. House with blue paint.'

He was far from believing this scenario impossible. A teenager needed less motive than any normal adult would, having an imperfectly formed connection with reality; half their world fantastic; half of it uncomprehended adult standards and exactments. Add to this the adolescent ego and the whole thing was on a short fuse.

He drew up near the blue-painted house, and getting out circled the car to open the door for Mrs Braun. She had already opened it, so he held it while she swung out a pair of slim muscular ankles.

'Right. Let's see what she's up to.'

The house was as stuffy as the salon, though cooler. He caught the same lingering scented chemical on the air. The hall, whose wallpaper was so busy as to look frantic, had pottery masks on the walls of Spanish and Jamaican heads. The blue satin festoon blinds in the lounge hung askew as if someone had got angry with them. A blue dralon sofa had resolutely scattered cushions in gold. Mrs Braun cast a sardonic glance around, as if she had reservations about the effect. He remembered that the house belonged to her mother.

About to offer him a drink, she said, 'Oh no, you're on duty, aren't you? Can't think how you lot manage. Not that you all do.' She poured herself a large whisky from a glittering drinks trolley that could have come from a film set, and drank it neat. The only effect was to make her eyes turn up briefly, like those of a doll. She turned towards the stairs and with an effortless rise in decibels called 'BEV! Come on down.'

Bone was not quite too deafened to hear another seamless echo from on high.

'*You* come up *here*.'

Mrs Braun turned to Bone with pride. 'You see? You better go up to her. I've been standing all day and I don't fancy those stairs.'

'Sorry. We have to play by the rules. Either she comes down or we both go up. I can't talk to her except in your presence.'

'You do play it straight, don't you? Okay.' She tipped the bottle into her glass again and headed for the stairs. A battle with her daughter was clearly not among her plans.

There had been a sound of rhythm, but now, perhaps hearing her mother's toiling tread on the thick pile, Bev beamed them in on a blare of heavy metal, drums pounding through the walls. Bone was lucky with Cha, whose liking for rock'n'roll did not demand full volume. To hearing-damage they entered a room whose black-painted walls and ceiling held posters of violently singing men with flying hair. Coloured lighting turned the planes of their faces bizarre in bulges of emerald and purple. On the floor Bev, couched with rump in the air, disregarded visitors. She had changed from her uniform into a magenta jump-suit. Folded pieces of card were piled beside her and he saw, astonished, that she was making Christmas cards. Werewolves might buy flowers for Mothers' Day.

Mrs Braun knew the drill. She lifted the arm of the record-player, swung it to 'off' and sat down on the crumpled bed, patting a space beside her for Bone to take. It was occupied in part by a one-eyed bear lying there mugged. Bone removed it and, holding it, sat down. Beverly sat up.

'Saw you last night,' she said truculently. 'I know who *you* are. What the fu—what the fuzz want now?'

'To know more about last night.'

'Like what? You could of asked me then.'

'Not without your mother's permission.'

'I don't need her permission to talk to you.'

'But I do.'

'I'd have been there,' said Mrs Braun, searching through

99

things on the bedside table, finding cigarettes and taking one, 'if I'd known you were doing your right part.'

'What happened to Mairi?' Bone asked.

Beverly shook her head in simple wonder.

It was a striking face. The skin, uniformly pale, was shown up by the shock of dyed-black hair. Some other oddness about her face made it both weird and vulnerable: she had no eyebrows.

'You were in Room Nine with the other girls,' he began.

'Prozzies. Right.'

'Never in my young days,' said Mrs Braun. 'We weren't supposed to know. Now they act them on stage in front of parents.'

'It's called progress, Ma. You must've heard of it. Let Cha's dad ask his questions or you'll get your collar felt for obstructing.' She snatched the bear, clasped him upside down to her notable bosom and sat back on her heels. 'Me and the other slags were meant to stay in there. Baa-Lamb kept trying to herd us back there.'

'So you were out in the passage quite a lot?'

'Could have been.'

'Whom did you see out there?'

'The Lamb. Fazileh. Anne Higgins. Sam MacGregor. Wally the wally, Old Acid Face and You-Done-It.'

'Give people their right names, Bev. How's Mr Bone to know who they are?'

'Charred Bone, that's how. Sweet Chariot.'

Mrs Braun's elbow nudged him and she said 'Tsk!' with enjoyment. Bone acknowledged, tacitly, that he knew Old Acid Face by saying, 'I thought Mr Sharpe was stationed on the other side of the stage.'

'Didn't stay there, did he? Round our side about three times, peeking to see his darling. It's a wonder—' and Beverly's face became suddenly empty—'that he didn't make a zonking great bulge in the backcloth.' The bear's leg as she reversed him protruded at hip level and was smacked down. She went on, 'Claire swanned about scattering sweetness.'

'Did Miss Fairlie speak to Mr Sharpe?'

'May have.'

'I must be precise. Do you mean you didn't see or hear them speak together?'

'Right. I didn't. He went in the D.S. but no joy.'

'You saw Mr Sharpe go into the D.S.'

'Yeh. He was out in a tick. He came and shut our door. When I opened it he was gone.'

'Did you see him go?'

'Nup. Could have gone back in the D.S. and—' she made a jab with the all-purpose bear. Her eyes were bright with interest.

'Did you hear voices in the D.S?'

'Too much row off the stage.'

'When did you next see Miss Fairlie?'

'Didn't.'

'Did you see Mr Sharpe again on that side of the stage?'

'No. *Heard* him, we all did, when Grue looked in. But she held the door and screeched for Baa-Lamb. She butted me right in the boozzi when I tried to see.'

'Christ,' said her mother. 'You didn't say. That's bloody dangerous.'

'No it's not. Old wives' tale. Doesn't give you cancer.'

'You needn't be so sure, girl. My Aunt Vi . . .'

Bone saw an unlikely thing on the wall, the famous flying ducks. It seemed probable that Beverly would have desecrated them in some way, and he looked below them for the flying turds. His imagination had let him down, though. An arc of scarlet drops trailed down towards the cutout silhouette of a man with a rifle by the skirting board.

Mrs Braun's anecdote found its end, to her emphatic nod.

'Did you help in the search for Miss Fairlie?'

'Went and looked in the D.S. window. Of course you can't see behind the demo bench so—' she shrugged. 'All very well for *you*, but I've never been that close to a murdered body and I never got to see it.'

'Morbid little monkey,' said Mrs Braun with a mouthful of smoke.

Bone wondered if the actual sight of Claire Fairlie would have dissipated the haze of dark fascination corpses held for the fortunate ignorant. Beverly asked, 'How's it feel, looking at them?'

The question was challenging. Bone, entitled to his reti-
cences, shrugged in his turn. 'One gets used to it,' he said with
casual untruth. 'Now, it was first realised that Miss Fairlie was
missing quite near the time she was to go on. What happened?'

'Sam MacG said she should be there ready, so the Lamb
went to knock at the D.S. No answer. Me and some others
went to look in the window, Alison or someone went for Miss
Dunne. Panic stations, Lamb off to search the bog, no Sugar
Plum. Kefuffle, little Higgins had gone on to announce Mrs
Trapse. Lamb going critical, hands to mouth, big hysteria
going into countdown.' The round shoulder rose. 'I got the
hat, took off me apron, went on.'

'I'd give an eye tooth to've seen it.'

'It was a great performance,' Bone said with sincerity. 'Beverly
took the stage like a trouper. I've seldom enjoyed a scene
more.'

'Drop dead,' Beverly said, crushing the bear on her thigh.
Her face had shut down. Mrs Braun said, 'That's not nice,
Bev.'

Bone could not recall the present vogue phrase for 'genuine'.
He said, 'On the level.'

A fugitive emotion brought Beverly's chin up and drew her
body straight. She said, 'Shit, it was all unrehearsed. Bad
notes like bloody confetti.'

'They don't know how to take compliments these days.
Kids are that ungracious.'

'Did you see anyone else round the building?'

'Peeping Tom, you mean? Peeping Harry. Dirty Harry the
Knicker Tweaker. Bet you he's got form somewhere as a
groper. Horrible but harmless, like all the men in school.
Sharpe hates kids, Herbert's gay, Harry can't get it up.'

'Bev!'

'I reckon him on "interfering". Feels up the first years and
like that.'

'Do you know that, Beverly? Has anyone told of an experience of that sort involving Harry Birch, in your hearing?'

'Mrs Pepper was on about it last year, someone had told her.
He wasn't got rid of. Then Pepper left and You-Done-It came

instead. He must have felt up Miss Mallett and she was so thrilled she gave him the job for life.'

'Bev. That's over the edge. That won't do. I won't have it.'

'Okay,' Beverly said indifferently.

'Just Harry Birch, then. No one else was around.'

'I didn't see him. Every prozzie in the place shouting "Someone's looking in!" I flipped my skirt. Give him an eyeful of knickers. Spread a little kindness.'

Mrs Braun choked on her cigarette. Recovering, her eyes astream, she said, 'She comes out with these things! Sometimes I don't know where to look.'

'Harry Birch did.'

'Was anyone outside when you went to look in at the D.S. window?'

'Didn't see anyone. Might not, though, with lights inside and all dark out.'

'Exactly what did you see when you looked in?'

Beverly treated this with a weary glance but, after running the worn fur of the bear's ear along her lips a few times, she raised her panda-painted eyes and said, 'The only thing was her make-up mirror stood up on the bench. I couldn't see the bench top so her make-up or whatever didn't show.'

'Any taps running? Drawers pulled out?'

She closed her lips on the ear and once again called up the scene. 'Nup. Not even blood on the blackboard. Nah, there was a teatowel on one of the grills.' Her hand indicated a ledge above eye level. 'Just thrown there it looked. Mrs Garland would've done her nut. Fire hazard. Big no-no.'

'Thank you, Beverly. You're observant.'

She looked more disgusted than pleased, but the pleasure was all Mrs Braun's. 'There now.' She stood up with Bone.

'Chuck me the ciggies,' Beverly said. As they descended, Marillion's decibels burgeoned.

Bone, as he got in his car again and jigged the keys into the ignition, considered whether the verve, the exhilaration of Mrs Trapse last night sprang from artistic delight, from chemical help, or conceivably in triumph at an act seen as justice, the removal of the betraying, fickle, usurping Sugar Plum Fairlie.

Sharpe, he thought. Sharpe was in the D.S., he came out

quickly to check who was about, shut the girls into their dressing-room and went back. Motive and opportunity. Sharpe had lied about watching her house.

He set off for the station.

She had got away. She had got away after all. There in the car at the traffic lights. He was guarded among other cars to the sound of horns of victory, and put his hands to the glass at her side and said her name. Her head turned, her face became her other face, her devil face, and her car flung him down. Though the road and the traffic island were allowed to hurt him, he could see the car as it went. Now he knew he was still following his duty because he had been shown the car. He had only to find it again. He would walk until he found her car, and then he could carry out his duty, finish what they said he was to do.

CHAPTER
9

The desk sergeant, facing a member of the public across the counter, greeted Bone with relief. He followed him round behind the filing stack and muttered, 'The Fairlie woman's sister down from Scotland. She's a bit of a tartar.'

'Name?'

'Mrs Edward Lawrence.'

'She's upset.' Bone, as he often did, stated rather than asked.

'It's not that, I'd say. Annoyed. Thought you'd want to know before you saw her. She seems to take the murder as arranged for her sole inconvenience.'

'Where's Inspector Locker?'

'He's on the phone.'

'We'll take the interview room rather than my office. Tell him, would you, when he's free?' From the sound of Mrs Lawrence, he would need another hand.

The woman waiting, her gloved fingers clicking the top of her handbag, fixed him with expectant disapproving eyes. She had a superficial likeness to her sister, but the dark hair was short and confined close to her head, the heart-shaped face was pointed, the mouth unsmiling and thin.

'This is Detective-Superintendent Bone, madam.'

'I'm in charge of Miss Fairlie's case. Shall we go where there's a little privacy? Any chance of some tea, Sergeant?'

'Can do, sir.'

He had hardly opened the door to the corridor when she

broke out. 'I went to her house. The man in the basement wouldn't let me in. He took it on himself to say he couldn't do it. I'd expected to stop there.' She had sufficient Scots accent to make it 'expectit'. 'If it's not my house now, it's my father's. I'd like to know what you want with it still. What do you need to do? You've not turned out that disgusting pair from the basement, so why can I not get in?'

'They are in a separate part of the house, Mrs Lawrence. Miss Fairlie's part is still being investigated.'

'That pair should be investigated. They imposed on Claire. She was far too good-natured, for ever befriending folk who only let her down.'

Opening the door for her, Bone reflected that some of the folk he'd talked to were of the opinion that Claire had let *them* down. Mrs Lawrence bustled ahead of him, glanced round with a sort of spiritual sniff, and sat down at the table. She had a plain wool overcoat, navy, and a navy felt hat of the Robin Hood style. Instead of a feather in the band it had a pheasant's claw, a horrid little trophy.

'Must I stay in a hotel, then? I've been travelling all day. Do the police pay expenses of those kept out of their own houses?'

'Were you asked to come, Mrs Lawrence?' He knew the answer.

'I was not. There was hardly the need to ask me. Common human feeling, family feeling, brought me.'

'If you had telephoned, we could have warned you that the house was not available.' What with Martin Grant making free with Fairlie's bed, and her sister ready to sleep there, it did not seem that anyone had morbid scruples about it.

'When will the funeral be?'

'We'll let you know, Mrs Lawrence. We can't say as yet.'

'What does it depend on?'

'I will ask the pathologist.'

There was a slight pause.

'It's a horrible thing,' she said in a suddenly muted tone. Though softer, there was still the note of reproach. Bone gathered that he was at the moment responsible for all that was wrong with Mrs Lawrence's world. 'We've never had any of the family, nor anyone we know of for that matter, meet such an end. My husband is very upset, very disturbed. What he'll say about keeping the body from the family I don't know.'

Her likeness to her sister, as Bone gravely watched her, appeared as if it showed through some intervening substance. Claire's face itself he had seen. Imagining it with the vitality that had been subtracted, a moving version of the photographs he had found in her house, he saw the same structure as this, but here restrained, fenced in, and with puffy flesh overlaying it.

A constable came in with two cups of tea. She waited for hers to be put down before her, disapproved of it slightly, and when the door had shut, said, 'What's been done, then? Have you arrested someone?'

'The investigation is continuing. We're hard at work, Mrs Lawrence.'

'But what's happening? Surely you have some idea?'

'Miss Fairlie wrote to you quite often.'

'Not regularly. She preferred writing to the telephone. She let us know about the marriage.'

Bone, with a sense of carpet retreating beneath his feet, asked, 'What did she say about it?' and drank tea.

'She let us know it would be next year. Edward was irritated that she was so unspecific. No doubt you can tell me more than she could be troubled to do.'

Sharpe had seemed to expect to marry Claire. Hazeley, still married, might be considering divorce.

'What's being *done*, Inspector?'

As Locker came in at this moment, he might suppose the question was being directed at him. Bone considered whether Mrs Lawrence's sense of righteousness might not be reflected, though with a difference, in Claire Fairlie's sense of superior judgement, her management of others for their own good, and her expectation of being admired.

Locker said, 'Sorry I wasn't available, sir,' glanced at her, and drew a chair up to a well-considered position between intrusion and detachment.

'This is Detective-Inspector Locker, assisting in the case. Mrs Edward Lawrence; Aimée Lawrence.' Letters in the house provided her name. She gave a sharp glance at him because of it. The untasted tea gathered scum before her.

'Who was she going to marry?' she demanded. 'It was the man at her school, wasn't it? The brilliant scholar. But they ran after her. "Two strings to my bow" she wrote me. A bonny girl like Claire! Plenty of men were after her. Since she was at school herself, she's never lacked for boys running after her.'

It was the first note of approval she had uttered, and spoken without envy, as if Claire's attractiveness were a family credit.

'She wrote of a scholar?'

'And there was another man, or more.' The navy bag thumped her lap. 'A crime of passion. He ought to be in custody.'

'It's public-spirited of you to offer this information, Mrs Lawrence. Whom did she name?'

'Name? Surely you know their names. You're the one on the spot, Mr Bone or Bone or whatever you like to call yourself. I thought the *police* were supposed to be well informed.' Clearly Bone did not fit this bill.

'We arrive at our information, Mrs Lawrence, by asking questions. Miss Fairlie did not say whom she intended to marry?'

'She did not. I've her letter somewhere. I couldn't lay hands on it before I came away. Edward is looking it out and he will send it to Claire's house. Where, I suppose, you'll impound it.'

'It would not be proper to impound correspondence addressed to you.' Bone did not rehearse the instances when it would be proper. 'I should be very interested to have any information that may have a bearing on the case, and you would, I'm sure, let me have such information. Miss Fairlie made a mystery of it all, I take it.'

'She would use initials, like a game. Claire was too apt to be frivolous over serious matters. She would do it to annoy me, I'm aware. I hold marriage to be a serious step.' She eyed them as if sure they would consider it a frivolous one. Bone experienced the ennui of having his natural beliefs authorised by a tedious woman. Her hands set to work again on her bag, clicking the clasp open and shut, open and shut. He saw that, although tired by her journey, she was full of a baffled energy that lacked anything to do. She needed to look through the house, sort belongings and furniture, arrange a sale, arrange her sister's burial . . .

'We can help you in one way,' he said. 'We have a list of accommodation, although it's not our job to find any and we are not allowed to make recommendations.'

'Is there a temperance hotel?'

'There is. I'll ask that one of the constables bring you the address.' He was glad to recall a very pleasant friend who invariably sought out temperance hotels. There were times when the *unco' guid* gave such things a bad name. Fair Temperance, you need no enemies.

He and Locker rose, and he uttered some condolences there had until now hardly seemed call for. Mrs Lawrence thanked him with dignity. 'I hope this matter is soon going to be resolved,' she added. 'Edward is most upset, very disturbed.' Whether this was to Edward's credit as a caring brother-in-law, or a hint that the police had better get their running-shoes on for fear of Edward's wrath, Bone did not care to guess.

As they returned to Bone's office, where details of the case, and pictures, had been left spread out after the last conference, Locker said, 'Who bit on a lemon, then?'

'I didn't need her at this point, did you? Still, who knows what the letter mayn't have.'

'If Edward's not too worked up to find it.'

Bone grinned, and at once took heart. The sister had depressed him. He sat down and said, 'Let's review the whole thing, Steve.'

'This Mrs Lawrence is pretty sure Fairlie did intend to marry, sir.'

'And Sharpe said she'd been going to marry him before Hazeley came along.'

'I didn't catch any word of marriage from Hazeley.'

'An affaire. Sometimes three evenings a week. Quite a warm affaire, though not passionate. But then Sharpe says that lately she'd been reviving relations with *him.*'

'We've only his word for it.'

'I've Beverly Braun's word, for what it's worth, that Sharpe had more opportunity than he claims to have had for talking to Fairlie, and therefore, for the murder. Let's go through it, Steve.'

They reviewed the list, which Bone had made under the

time-honoured headings, Opportunity, Motive. Every one of those on the Prompt side of the stage was listed under Opportunity. They read:

> Ian Sharpe
> Barbara Lambert
> Amanda Wallace
> Ursula Dunne
> Fazileh Rashidi
> Samantha MacGregor
> Anne Higgins
> Beverly Braun
> Prudence Grant
> Caroline Timmins
> Tanya Whitby
> Katherine Hazeley
> Alison Settle
> Emma Jones
> Anita da Silva
> Harry Birch
> Martin Grant
> ? unknown

Against only Sharpe was there a tick under Motive, with queried ticks for Martin and Beverly. 'Any possible connection of Kat Hazeley and her father's affaire with the Sugar Plum?'

'Jealous, you mean? Felt herself dropped for the sake of her Dad? More likely to gun for *him*, I'd've thought, if he hits her.'

'Suppose Sharpe fabricated this reconciliation that Fairlie started lately, and there was still a big thing going with Hazeley, he's still the prime villain. But I'm looking at blood patterns. That's still the problem. He's the only one with blood on his clothes, but whoever did it, if there's any blood at all, must have a good deal.'

'Any possible motive for Lambert?'

'None known. Fairlie was after her job.'

'Then there's this Ursula Dunne. She's a nice woman to talk to, but the girls say Fairlie was always putting her down.'

'Can be nasty,' said Bone, to whom it had happened for long years with one superior officer, 'but murder? And then, character? It's not a certain indication, but the Dunne girl didn't read like that to me. Who else is there?'

'The Samantha kid was fixed to the prompt book all the time, she saw nothing and didn't even know Fairlie was missing. Thought she was just letting Braun go on. She didn't know it *was* Braun till she started to sing. "Ever so surprised" she was, when she heard the voice and looked up. As to opportunity, she had none, she was in sight of the actors the whole time. We could cross her off. The other girls can't account for each other, they were seething to and fro, going across the playground to the toilet there, visiting the other dressing-rooms or the wings and getting chased back, creating about this Peeping Tom, all they're short of is a speck of motive among the lot of them. The only thing they're a bit quiet about is this Beverly. Well, Alison Settle says "Bev would do absolutely anything but not kill someone."'

'An ambiguous statement.'

Locker turned back through the transcript. 'Here's Anita da Silva, she's an older girl: "Miss Fairlie was pretty mean to Bev, but all Bev said was, 'That's life, isn't it?' and she didn't seem that bothered." And she said to Mairi Leggatt, "My turn yesterday, you today, so who's tomorrow?"—which is hearsay, not evidence, but it gives an atmosphere.'

'Their general opinion is that Beverly would not do it. Only Mairi Leggatt was convinced that she probably had.'

'Mairi Leggatt being under the influence at the time of the accusation.'

'Oh yes. Now Martin. He was round the back at the possible time. He was full of the way he'd been treated, Fairlie laughing at him after drawing him on, and from his account she had certainly done that. Now you'd be more detached in his case. I've known him for years.'

'It'd be easier if that stab hadn't been, like, a lucky shot. It didn't take a lot of strength or knowledge. Anyone could have done it. It could have been chance or it could have been clever, but either way it hit a fatal spot. Sharpe is still the front runner however you look at it.'

'He went across at least once to see Fairlie. He's obsessed about her. He expected to marry her until Hazeley showed.'

Locker said, 'Pull him in and put it to him?'

Bone drew his hands down over his face. He looked at the names.

'I don't know why not, Steve. Nine times out of ten it's the obvious bloke who's the one.'

'You're not for it this time?'

'How good is Hazeley's alibi?'

Locker's eyebrows shot upwards. However, he said, 'He was at Mr and Mrs Samuel Pearsall's with three other guests by seven forty-five. He was a bit late, he said he'd had an overseas phone call from a client in New York who's got an eye on Herne Hall as a conference centre. The operator gives that call as coming through at seven eighteen, lasting fourteen minutes. I don't see him getting from his house to the school, round the back, stabbing Fairlie and getting to the Pearsalls' in eighteen minutes, give or take a few. Even twenty, if Mrs Pearsall wasn't exact.'

'It's not realistic. If it was premeditated and if he knew exactly where she'd be and if he could count on not being seen by his daughter and her pals in the passage—'

'But he had a fair excuse if he was seen, saying hallo to his daughter.'

'I'm fantasising, Steve; suppose he had a rendezvous with her, she said, "I'll be in the D.S. room at about seven thirty . . ." it's over the top. He looks to be in the clear. It's like the sort of time-table killing you read about. Better try the drive tonight at the same hour, Steve, see how long it takes. I've no expectation and it proves nothing if it can be done.'

Locker said, 'I don't like the man either,' and Bone glanced up and smiled.

'You're right, Steve. Dead right. It's reprehensible. He's a child-beating bully but we don't so easily fit him up for this. Incidentally, last June his wife reported him to the NSPCC and Kat denied he ever hit her. The housekeeper says he spoils the girl if anything, and the answer's a lemon.'

'Didn't Treasure say the daughter admitted to Fairlie that her father hit her?'

Bone shook his head, mouth tight. 'I checked the report. She denied it to the Inspector from the Society. No case.'

Locker grimaced. Remembering Hazeley's confident smile and overbearing ease of manner, Bone sighed. 'This is an unsatisfactory world and it's run without consideration for moral justice. Don't you wonder if God regrets the bargain He made with Noah? A deluge or so might clear the place up a bit. I'm over-reacting, of course. What's a clout on the face to a nice girl who loves her father?'

Locker swung an arm up—to look at his watch. 'I'll get along to Hazeley's and do that drive.'

Bone, startled, stared at his own watch. 'No wonder I'm hungry. Cha will be wondering. I never phoned her.'

'I'll ring you at home, shall I, about the timing?'

'Right. I'd like to know.'

Around eight o'clock, when Bone and Charlotte were busy with fried cheese sandwiches, Locker telephoned.

'I made it, sir. Stood outside the back of the school for two minutes, got to Pearsall's gate just on ten to. I'm only glad the traffic squad weren't around, that's all. I was driving with due care and attention, but at a hell of a bat. It did come to me that Hazeley's the type to drive like that as a habit, but even if he does it's no help to us.'

'Thanks, Steve. We'd best see him again. Goodnight.'

Hazeley, however, could not be seen. He was dining with friends in Lewes, said his housekeeper, and staying overnight. He did not expect to be back until mid-day, as he had business in the area. His secretary would know what it was. She gave the secretary's number without demur.

Miss Pellew did know all about tomorrow's business, viewing a fire-damaged property with the loss adjuster, an appointment made last week. Bone thanked her, relieved to be satisfied that Hazeley was not purposely unavailable.

It didn't need, he thought as his eyes watched television, to be neatly premeditated at all. He might have zipped round to the school to see Claire Fairlie, to make a date perhaps, and she might have enraged him in one minute flat and he, in a room full of weapons, seized—but what was she doing while he looked in drawers for a knife? Laughing? Making up? Her hands had been empty, not clutching a lipstick or mascara brush. And somehow, the picture of Hazeley stabbing her in the back didn't gel. He was a bludgeon man, or a throat-grabber. Personal violence, not a knife. Or, if a knife, face to face, to see his effect, to triumph.

And I may be wrong, Bone conceded to his own doubts. We judge all the time but not infallibly. I have to trust my judgements, though. That's what my job is about. Go by the facts and then, on the edge of the facts, are the intangibles. They are facts too. I can't neglect Hazeley because method and timing are unlikely. I can't neglect Sharpe because, in that first interview, he convinced me.

At this point the persistent rustling behind him was punctuated by a hissed, 'No, Ziggy!' and he nearly turned his head. Charlotte was finishing his present-wrapping and all turning of the head was interdicted. The cat Ziggy, a Rum Tum Tugger, saw his part in this clearly: to kill the wrapping paper.

On the screen, a charming jackal family, whose gambols Bone had been watching without seeing them, suddenly began to tuck into their mother's prey. As they tore at the belly, the gazelle's head jerked. God, Bone thought, it's alive. Mother Nature. Young Ziggy's ancestors must have behaved just like that.

'Have you got your prezzie for me yet?' Charlotte asked.

'Lord, am I supposed to give you presents as well as keep you? Is there no end to the expense? Oh well, a packet of sweets will have to do.'

'You *have* got it,' said Charlotte, pleased. Her fidgetting and swearing had stopped, so the present must be wrapped. He felt Ziggy under his chair, and a moment later his trouser-leg was being worried, while hind paws pushed off against his ankle. It's no good killing my leg, he apostrophised the muscular fur bundle as he lifted it free. At least you're a domestic animal, or you'd be pulling your prey to bits all over the cave floor instead of coming running when you hear the opening of a tin.

Ziggy had a gentleman's agreement with Bone. He was Charlotte's cat, but he would use her father as a make-do. He fell against Bone's stomach, flung up a leg and got on with his laundry.

Charlotte came to sit on the sofa, stretched out. 'I am ek—sauce—ted. I've done all the ones for Aunt Alison and Derek and Don.'

'Oh God yes, they have to be early, don't they?'

'Record tokens will do. I can get them.'

Bone fished out his wallet. 'Thanks.'

'Going to be a nice Christmas,' she said. 'Just us.' His sister was going to her in-laws with her husband and the boys. She had offered to take Charlotte along, but Charlotte had become incoherent at the very thought. Bone was beginning to be convinced that she enjoyed the prospect of a Christmas shared with him, and that he had suffered the two previous ones with Alison for Charlotte's sake in vain.

Ziggy turned on his back, laid his head between Bone's knees and stared at Cha upside down.

CHAPTER
10

He drove with the car heater full on. It did not help.

The shop broadcasting carols had muted them a good deal, presumably in answer to popular demand, but the information that it came upon the midnight clear, that glorious song of old, of angels bending near the earth, reached Bone as he passed slowly. Since childhood he had seen those angels as very precarious, doubled up in the sky to reach harps of gold at arms' length. Not until a few years ago had he given it thought again, and realised that 'bending near ... to touch' did not necessarily mean that the harps were almost inaccessible. An old vision should have dissolved with the knowledge, but it persisted. The angels still, in his imagination, leant in Anglo-Saxon attitudes down the night sky.

Locker, refreshed after some sleep, had news.

'Talking to Miss Cantrell at the school, and she says Harry Birch gave notice last Friday and withdrew it Tuesday morning. Any significance, would you say?'

'Could ask him why. If it is significant, he won't tell us.'

'There's been a few words from the girls, about him peeking for instance, and the girls say he likes to get his hand on their thighs. He's not been known to do worse though he talks of it. They think he's a bit of a joke.'

'Does Miss Mallett know?'

'Well, didn't ask her. Now this has come to light about his notice, it might mean something. I reckoned you might want ...'

'I'm going to see Sharpe again this morning and I'd better see Birch, and have a word with Miss Mallett.'

'Birch comes from the Midlands. He wouldn't have got a job at this school without references of course, but suppose he's been bothering little girls up at Brum?'

'Form, do you think?'

'He's not done anything too bad here. Behaving, you might say. Don't want to stir anything up, but if he's given to the habit then you know the pattern.'

Bone knew. Good behaviour for a while encouraged the feeling of security. He'd start again, go a little farther. For some flirty children it would be all a game. Some would get a shock. Then he could go too far. Some child would have an experience she'd never forget. It might be an intimate fumble, it might be exposure. It could get as far as rape and a lifelong scar.

He sucked his cheek, thinking, then, 'Yes. Try Brum, call around. At any rate I'll let Harry know we're wise to him, and tell Miss Mallett. She's got to know.'

'So he'll get the sack and move on.'

'M'm. We can't help it. Protect the kids in our parish. If he goes for the little ones . . .'

But he thought of Charlotte.

Prayers were in progress. He heard the hymn, and then the measured chanting of the Lord's Prayer, and he stood still in the entrance hall while it lasted. Fazileh Rashidi and two younger girls stood by the Hall doors to go in. When they did, he set off for Harry Birch's den. Bone's religion was an amalgam of respect and cynicism. During Charlotte's coma after the smash he had prayed without ceasing, desperately, lying in his own hospital bed or beside her in a wheelchair. Now, when she made some particular triumphant step (could say 'then' or 'I'll', could announce that her hip hadn't hurt for three days), he gave thanks. This seemed an involuntary act connected with himself at a deeper level than thought, for though he believed, he avoided thinking about it.

Harry Birch stood up, or got down, from a high wooden stool covered with a dun-coloured greasy object like the corpse

117

of a cushion, and he trundled forward a mended chair, saying, 'What can I do for you? It's the police innit?'

Bone didn't sit, he leant on the chair back and said, 'Touching little girls, Harry.'

Harry's face was a series of bulges—cheeks, eyelids, lips, chins. It all went rigid. 'I never.'

'You married, Harry? Got any of your own?'

'No.'

'It won't do, Harry. Don't touch.' Bone looked at the neat work on the chair, the sanded finish. 'I don't want you to lose your job. Wouldn't any place but a school be better?'

Birch was silent. He wore a curious look, defensive but puzzled. 'I like it here. I've done no harm. You hear me? No harm. Your lot come chasing me, hounding me down, how'm I to live?'

'Get a job away from children.'

'I never hurt one. Never. I swear it. Who tells you I did? Anyone say to you Harry Birch hurt a child, they're a liar.'

'There's hurt and hurt, Harry. You get a buzz out of something, it seems harmless to you, a bit of fun. For some girls it's no more than that either. For others it's a sickener. And it leads to real trouble.' He raised his eyes and gave Harry a straight stare. 'As you know.'

The pouchy face flushed. 'God, don't leave anyone alone, do you? What happened, they pass the word from Selly, did they?'

'No.'

A light dawned. His eyes widened and then his face fixed into a curious blankness, as if he put on innocence. He said nothing, but Bone had seen that moment of comprehension. Birch thought he knew how Bone was onto him. That the children had complained? Surely he always knew they might, and it could hardly be a revelation or a surprise.

'Well?' Bone asked.

'Yeh. Well.' He was now shutting down, truculent. 'I'm not saying any more. You lost me my job.'

'You lost yourself your job, Birch.' His tone had altered in keeping with that challenge. 'You're the one that feels them up.'

118

'I never did one of them any harm. Not one.'

'You don't know what you do to them. Get that into your head. It's nothing to you but it's not nothing to them. Look at yourself, Birch. Are you love's young dream? Are you the right person to give a child her first taste of sex? Keep off them.'

Birch glowered.

Later Miss Mallett listened with pursed mouth. She thanked him. 'This is something I ought to have known. How did the information come to light, Mr Bone?'

'A group of younger girls stopped Inspector Locker and told him.'

Miss Mallett drew herself up a little. 'I cannot help wondering why none of the staff was approached by them first.'

'Apparently no parents complained either. Girls are very secretive creatures, aren't they?'

'Birch gave in his notice last Friday. He withdrew it yesterday. He came in and said that circumstances had altered and he did not need to move away from the area after all, so that he could continue next term.' She paused and gazed out of the window. Bone covertly mopped his face. Miss Mallett's greenhouse was no place for a man in winter clothes. 'I regret this, extremely,' she said. 'Birch is very good at his job. He's the first satisfactory caretaker we have had for ten years, and now ... It's very, very disturbing that this has been happening and no one's been told.'

Bone could not advise her; nor could he say that her remark about Birch's notice and its withdrawal might indeed be very significant. The girls might well have confided in the popular, the understanding Miss Fairlie.

Birch had suddenly become a runner.

Bone surprised Miss Cantrell, the school secretary, by making instant sense of the vast timetable on her wall, locating Mr Sharpe without help, and saying 'Two-D. Aren't the second year out today?'

'Yes, Mr Bone. Mr Sharpe should be free.'

'Thank you. I'll see if he's in his room.'

A vigorous singing practice was going on in the Hall. Bone skirted its doors and took the passage beyond it, arriving at the door marked *Deutsches Zimmer*. He looked in. Mr Sharpe raised his round, neat head, twitched at his spectacles as if to assure himself that his sight was not at fault and said 'Come in, come in,' rising to stand behind the desk. 'Yes, yes, Mr Bone. What can I do for you?'

Bone sat on one of the front-row desks and Sharpe subsided into his chair. Despite the little platform on which the staff desk stood, Bone had the advantage of height. He uttered the platitudes about checking details. Behind Sharpe's head a poster of Neuschwanstein graced the wall, its fantastic towers among the fox red autumn treetops. Sharpe, seeing Bone looking at something, turned to ascertain what it was.

'To call a man mad for building that betrays a view of sanity that is quite Prussian,' he said. The remark, delivered in a censorious tone, did not seem to be meant humorously.

'Jealousy, do you think? That he could realise his fantasies while they had to stick to politics? While they even had to run the country?'

'You know the story.'

'I've been there,' Bone nodded at the poster and went on before Sharpe could speak. 'You said when we were talking before that you wanted to marry Claire Fairlie. Did you actually propose to her?'

The round eyes behind the glasses stared, accusing Bone of cruel bad taste. However, he said, 'Not directly. I made a remark that was deliberately ambivalent. However, she took my meaning immediately and was quite honest. She said that she had no feelings that matched what mine apparently were. She was romantic. Women, I suppose, tend to be and she was one of the least practical of women. Her judgement was immature. The poor girl—' he glanced at his own hand that fidgetted with a stick of chalk in the desk's groove, a hand powdered with chalk as was his tweed jacket, like a badge of his profession. 'Claire was attracted by that brute Hazeley. I'm suprised that he is still at liberty. He has no control whatever. It's obvious that he . . .' But Sharpe could not bring himself to say 'killed her'.

'Control is what some murderers conspicuously possess, Mr

Sharpe. Besides, there is no evidence that he was anywhere near at the time.'

Sharpe's fingers flicked away this piece of irrelevance, as if evidence or the provision of it was Bone's business.

'There was Motive, Superintendent. He saw she was playing with him. He knew she was seeing me once more. Where there is motive there is always a means.'

Bone smiled. 'I don't know whether your theory would make police work infinitely more simple or immeasurably more complicated.'

'Are you a University man, Superintendent?'

Surprised, Bone regarded the little man stolidly. 'No, Mr Sharpe. If we take—'

'You have a quite scholarly rhythm of speech sometimes.'

Feeling disinclined to take up this gauntlet of intellectual snobbery, Bone had to stop himself from deliberately exaggerating the Kentishness of his tongue as he went on.

'I would have expected that, following your reasoning, Mr Hazeley would be more likely to have murdered *you*, Mr Sharpe.'

The eyes accused Bone once more. Had Sharpe long ago, as a toddler, turned those round reproachful eyes on his mother, and pulled his mouth's corners down, until she also felt guilty, as Bone did, without reason? Had that look irritated Claire?

'Me?' There was a pause. Then Sharpe's lips, that had often the appearance of having to open against his will, minced the reply, fastidiously under his moustache. 'It is true that he hated my what are vulgarly called "guts".' A spasm moved his face. Perhaps he recognised, as Bone did, that, businessman or schoolmaster, the animal under it all has the gut. The visceral reaction causes all the trouble. With true animals the matter is settled more simply: of two tom cats gurgling threats at each other on a wall, one has usually the sense to back, very slowly and cautiously, out of range in time. Animal rivals don't often kill.

A knock, and the door opened to admit, precipitately, two smallish girls, one holding out a gym skirt, the other nursing an armful of objects and clothing.

'Oh I'm sorry. We're going round with the lost property.'

They shut themselves out, with a burst of helpless giggles perhaps at the idea of either Bone or Mr Sharpe laying eager claim to the garment.

'So that Claire Fairlie had not agreed to marry you.'

'She had not.'

'Or to marry Michael Hazeley.'

He saw no shock in the face. 'She did not say so. No, I think not. It may be that the subject never arose between them. He is still married. She was vulnerable, you know. My natural cynicism benefited from her eternal optimism, and also I could try to protect her from committing herself so blindly to every cause that presented itself.'

'Do you know of any of her dealings about Harry Birch?'

'Birch? No!'

On the side of the staff desk that faced the class, incised and inked in, were the words I HATE SHARP. If Sharpe knew of this and was indifferent, if he knew of the mis-spelling of his name, Bone did not pursue. It might be diplomatic, in such a context, to allow the spelling to show ignorance. Yet Bone for an instant imagined Sharpe tutting, and scratching in an E in red ink.

He stood up. Sharpe said, 'What dealings with Birch?'

'One of the causes she took on. Thank you, Mr Sharpe.'

He went out, and made his way back to the secretary's office. At her door, he stood for a moment and rubbed his face. It was lucky that most homicides had an obvious solution. A member of that dangerous entity, the family, was so often the confessed or obvious killer, or one had only to track down a known person. These nebulous mysteries teased and tried him.

The door opened. Booted and wrapped, a sheaf of letters in her hands, the secretary appeared. He had barely time to straighten up, and wondered if she had seen his gesture of weariness. She said gaily, 'Off to the post! Did you want anything? To find someone else?'

'If you are going out, I'll use your telephone.'

'The grey one. The green I've switched through to Miss Mallett as I'm out.' She waved the letters and bobbed away out of the main doors, humming.

Locker had not heard yet from Selly Oak. Bone told him what Birch had admitted. 'You could call it "dishonest handling".' Locker chuckled at the term. 'It seems to be no more, Steve. It's enough. But whether Fairlie knew or not, I couldn't say. He wouldn't let on. From his silence I think she did. I've an hour before my appointment with Hazeley. I'll get a bite and a coffee.'

They had a word about other business, and then Bone rang off and went out into the entrance hall, buttoning his coat against an unwilling foray into the December day.

It had been a surprise to the staffroom that Mrs Lambert called-in-sick that day. At least the second year were out on a Workshop trip to Chilham, with Mrs Winant and Mrs Cartwright. Grizel Shaw, who had a 'free' anyway, and now an extra one, and was out shopping, decided that 'flu ought not to be left solitary. Lambie had never spoken of friendly neighbours, so that she might need some shopping done. Grizel turned off in her little car towards Mrs Lambert's street.

Impossible to envisage a Mr Lambert. Did he die? Were they divorced? Neither Lambie nor I ever speak of our ex's. I am not the one to keep my appendix in a glass bottle on the bedside table or anywhere else. If Lambie has the scars of marital struggle, she has kept them under bandages, and good luck to her. Yet I can't imagine her with a man. I can't imagine what kind of man would be hers. Perhaps that was the trouble.

The luck of living in the modern world! We don't have to live with our mistakes. Not so long ago, hardly a hundred years, I'd have been stuck with Lewis. Perhaps I'd have been signing the poison book at the chemist's, to get rid of that rat. Or would I have grabbed a knife in one of our rows, or would he?

Like Claire's death.

She nearly swerved. Her hands jerked on the wheel. It was two days ago and it seemed stitched into one's life, some process in the subconscious like the body's defences, of scar tissue, or callosities, prevented one's awareness of it all the time.

Once Nicola Garland had pinned up on the staffroom notice-board: *Never think you are indispensable. Your absence is as noticeable as the hole left in water when you take out your hands.*

Will my own death be like that? Whom do I matter to?

Well, here was the street she wanted. Baa-Lamb hadn't ever been away until now. In two years, that was quite a record. She was one of those who reproached one's own occasional absences by staggering in with high temperatures and hacking coughs so as 'Not to let anybody down', when everyone wished they would stay home and not be so generous with their germs. Poor Lambie must be half dead not to be at school during this time of crisis. Wally had sidled up to Grizel that morning and said, 'It must look so funny to the police.' Wally had enough bees in her bonnet to supply a whole orchard full of hives. Wonder you didn't hear her buzzing yards away. The idea of the police being struck by the humour of Lamb's absence was one of her best.

There was a line or two in the Charlotte's fathers face that suggested he wasn't immune to humour, of course.

Well, here was number twenty-eight and she could actually park outside. Where did Lambie keep her car? Did she run to hire of a garage? The sand Escort wasn't in sight. Grizel climbed out. Curtains shut in the first floor; poor creature. Hilary Tudor had said it was a first floor-flat. The cold bit hands and face. After that storm the weather had turned sharply colder. It was to be hoped Lambie had adequate heating. Three bells: Nicholson, Lambert, Parker. She rang the middle one.

Nothing. Of course, here was poor Lamb in bed. It might not be such a good idea to disturb her. Grizel stamped her boots. The entryphone stayed dumb. She ought not to have thought of getting Lamb out of bed, but too late now. She raised her face to those first-floor curtains and saw them twitch shut. The door, after a moment, buzzed and clicked. She pushed it. The entryphone said metallically, 'Do please be sure it's shut.' Grizel went in, and shut the door with care.

Mrs Lambert, at the door of the first floor-flat, was pale, rather wild-eyed, in a pink Acrilan dressing-gown furled and clutched tight around her. She took Mrs Shaw by the arm and seemed to tweak her through the door. 'I daren't risk the cold. Come in. How nice, how kind of you.'

'With my "free" and the second year being out, I've time. What shopping do you need? You get back into bed, my dear.' Almost awkwardly she used the common address, because she had never yet called Mrs Lambert by her first name, and the diminutives were not used by the staff to her face. She wondered if she were the first of them to see where this reclusive woman lived.

'No, I'm—I'm sitting up. I dislike being in bed.'

The room was stuffy, the air circulated by the fan heater imprisoned within the walls, smelling of defeat and sadness, of not quite fresh clothes and of old upholstery, yet, oddly enough, not of illness. She knew the smell of a sickroom and it was not here. Thick, lined chintz curtains, cabbage roses blowsily proliferating over them, showed a tiny chink of daylight. The bed's cover, also chintz, was half off and the bedclothes pulled up but rumpled as if she had been sitting there. She had no medicines, aspirin or water-glass, only the lamp whose pink shade cast a mendacious rosy glow, beside an alarm clock like the voice of conscience, a surprising small woolly dog and a framed photograph.

As an effort at establishing contact with Mrs Lambert, Grizel picked this up. Mrs Lambert made some hasty movement and then stood with hands clasped on the pink cloth at her throat.

'Is this your family?'

She made an acquiescent sound.

'Aren't you like your father!'

'Yes. Yes, I am.'

'And your brother? He's more like your mother, isn't he? Except his hair's only slightly red, not as much as yours. I've always envied hair your colour. Perhaps I'll dye mine red one day. Not just now, with the Head's ban on dyeing. What does your brother do? Does he teach too?'

'He—no. He's dead.'

The irrational guilt one always felt at this particular social mishap made her rattle the photograph down on the table with an apology and condolence. Perhaps he had died recently. She turned to Mrs Lambert, ready to speak, and met a fixed stare, suspicious, almost hostile.

'I really don't need anything,' Lambie was saying. 'I have not wanted to eat, and I've got plenty here. Enough for a siege.' She looked, in her defiant stance, as if that was indeed what she was prepared for, in her little fortress, guarded by the woolly dog and the wall of books.

'Will you be back this term, do you think? It's such a short time left.'

'No! Not at this rate, I mean. My temperature is very high. I don't want to give this to everyone for Christmas.'

Mrs Shaw could perfectly well recollect Lambie coming in conscientiously every day last March in a vile state of health and giving *her* 'flu for Easter. This was a change of policy, and there could be no doubt it was for the better.

'Yes, you should certainly nurse it. Are you really better out of bed, though? With a high temperature?'

'I know what's best for myself,' said Mrs Lambert, in so forbidding a tone that it amounted to pulling rank.

'What will you do about Christmas?' As she spoke, she caught sight of an airline bag, under a chair, with a sweater's arm supplicatory over its side. Mrs Lambert followed her glance and turned pink, as if caught out getting ready for holiday when term was still ending and her colleagues still at work. Grizel wondered suddenly if she meant to leave before term ended, if the illness were an excuse.

'Oh, I'm thinking of going—somewhere—somewhere warm. To the sun. When I'm better. To recover.'

Grizel hadn't pictured the Lamb as likely to go flitting off to the Bahamas for her turkey and mince pies. People were very certainly not what you thought they were. This cheerless little refuge was not what you'd expect for a woman with Lamb's salary. As she turned, she could see through another small room, a kitchen-diner, to a barred glass-panelled door giving onto a flight of steps that must lead to the garden. One ought to say how nice the place was; but it wasn't.

'It's very cosy,' she said. 'Are you sure there isn't anything, though, that I can get for you?'

'Nothing. No. Nothing at all. It's very kind,' said Mrs Lambert repressively.

'Should I bring anything from school? Books or things from your office? Or take in reports?'

'My reports are already with Miss Cantrell. There's nothing. I could come in during the holidays if I find there are things I need. There is nothing I can think of, thank you.'

'Look, can't I make you some coffee?' Grizel was aware of being officious, of forcing help where it was not welcome, and she turned hurriedly to the other door and opened it on the kitchen-diner. She went in. A small eating-booth was fitted into one corner. A sink, a cooker, a fridge, a window with curtains closed—

'No, no!' Mrs Lambert was saying. 'I don't *want* anything!'

Mrs Shaw turned. The Lamb was out of sight and, when she went back, she found her on the bed, her feet drawn under her, in the corner.

'Please understand I want nothing. You must go.'

'Mrs Lambert—Barbara—can't I help you? What's wrong?'

The eyes stared. 'It's not safe.' If a whisper could be a shriek, this was it. Disturbed at her disturbance, Grizel reached out to touch her, but she flinched back.

'I'm sorry. I don't mean to upset you.'

'I'm perfectly all right,' said Mrs Lambert. The only thing to do was to accept this patent lie.

'Very well. But—Barbara—let me leave you my phone number. If there is anything, if there should be something I could do, call me. Please believe me, you can call on me.'

'Yes-yes.' The poor woman was only anxious that her visitor should go. Grizel wrote her number on a scratch-pad on the shelf-desk.

'I'll let myself out. You keep warm and—try to relax.'

A meaningless involuntary smile answered her own. As she looked back from the door, Mrs Lambert gasped, 'Very kind.'

She descended the narrow stairs, thinking: *it won't do, it won't do at all*. This wasn't 'flu. Something very peculiar was going on. I can let myself out. I had no idea what I was letting myself in for.

As she drove, she thought, had Claire's death simply

unhinged the poor woman? If her brother's death were recent, and of course she might be quite recently widowed or divorced ... but I'm making things up now. 'It's not safe!' What wasn't safe? She's positively hiding in there. What's she afraid of? The murderer? Does she believe it's someone who has it in for teachers? Are we all in danger?

I'm being ridiculous. That poor woman, though, is definitely not in her right mind.

CHAPTER
11

She arrived at school to find Mr Bone's dark green car in her parking-space. Instantly, her problem was solved.

Bone, accosted by Mrs Shaw in the entrance hall, had been a little regretting that he had no reason to see her this morning, and the regret surprised him. The Siamese-cat eyes, so alive, almost on a level with his, distracted him from what she was saying now that she was, suddenly, before him, and he agreed to something without quite taking in what it was. She wore a black slouch hat and a shaggy fake fur coat in verdigris green.

'I don't know if I'm putting too much importance to it, but I don't think I am.' She led the way, pulling the hat from her pale hair. Round them the school hummed with lessons, a sudden rat-tat-tat of chalk on a board, distant singing, voices at random, a burst of laughter from one classroom, a scolding next door. They climbed wide stairs paved in grey terrazzo, and crossed a small landing. She ushered him into the Biology room.

'Won't you sit down? No, have the chair, those stools are deadly uncomfortable.'

'I'll park myself here, then.' He sat on one of the white tables. Two benches, with gas taps perched like dangerous insects, crossed the back of the room. In front were two rows of the white desks. Mrs Shaw plugged a kettle in, took off her coat showing a sweater of brilliant patchwork in orange, flame, tawny and rust, and unlocked a cupboard.

'I have to keep the bikkies locked away or the girls help themselves.'

'Things have changed. I can't see myself nicking biscuits from any of our schoolmasters.'

'Oh it's Marxism,' she said. 'Property is theft. That's everybody's philosophy these days.'

What a difference between Scot and Scot. Mrs Lawrence's accent was the grinding of pebbles, Mrs Shaw's like water running over them.

The tall windows overlooked the playground, where Miss Dare's voice urged, 'Mark!' and 'Jump for it, Emma!' This room must be above the D.S., still shut although his team had left it. Mrs Garland and Miss Mallett had decided it should not be used again this term.

He glanced at the words on the blackboard and looked away. There was an embarrassment, for him though perhaps not for a biologist, in 'rectum', 'faeces' and 'sphincter' if not in 'peristalsis' and 'colon'. A wall-chart on dentition was safe. Below it, a cut-away model of the human ear stood on a shelf beside a dog's skull.

She sniffed the coffee mugs and, seeing him notice, smiled. 'They use bleach in the kitchens. These are all right, though.' She spooned granules and poured, wreathing herself in steam. Milk came from the lab fridge.

She provided him with the lid of the biscuit box for a plate and saucer, and sat down, sideways to her desk. Her hair had been ruffled by the hat.

'I'm bothered over Mrs Lambert, Superintendent, and it came to me that I'd do well to tell you.'

'I heard she's got 'flu.'

'Well, I'm not so sure she has. I've just been round to her flat. I think she is maybe frightened of something. What it is I don't know, but I don't think she is ill. Mind you, I can't be sure. She didn't want me to touch her.'

'Tell me about it.'

'I'd some time I was using for a bit of shopping, so I went round to see could I do anything for her. I don't know her well, I don't think any of us does, but she's not been away ever in two years until now and so I thought she must be really bad. There's an entryphone so she'd no need to come down, but she didn't speak, she looked to see who it was before she opened the door. And she was dressed. She'd a dressing-gown on but she was dressed under it. Well, perhaps she felt cold, and she said she disliked being in bed, but every time I've had 'flu, horizontal was the only bearable way. No tablets around, either, and no sign of headache or pains or lassitude. She stood watching me, and she was very tense and nervous. I can't explain what the atmosphere was like.'

She was frowning now. Her lashes dipped to her cheek against the steam as she drank. 'Well then, I offered to make *her* some coffee and I went into the kitchen. It was like lighting a fuse! She whipped away onto the bed and cried "It's not safe!"'

'"It's not safe"?'

'That's right.'

'What was there in the kitchen?'

'That's what I can't make out. The usual things, cooker and fridge and sink. Cupboards. One of those dining nooks, and a fire-escape or garden door. She'd drawn the curtains over the window in there too. Did I say she'd the curtains drawn? But you would if you had 'flu. There was daylight through the glass of that door. I can't think why that would have frightened her. It was barred, after all.'

'She seemed to hide when *you* went in there.'

'I can't tell you,' she said, her eyes puzzled, 'how very strange she was.'

'We still have a murderer at large,' he said. 'Could she be afraid that she's next? Do you know of any connection at all between her and Miss Fairlie?'

'Bar that Fairlie fancied her job as Deputy Head. Though I wouldn't have it for seven times the pay. Lambie—' she suddenly smiled—'Mrs Lambert is good at it. She can organise, and she can keep the peace amongst us. Claire would have liked the power but I'm not so sure she could have handled the responsibility. It's been striking me how very reserved Mrs Lambert is. We don't know about her family. Perhaps Miss Mallett does. There was a photograph by the bed and—I made a gaffe—I talked of the brother, said he was like her, and it turns out he's dead.'

'Anyone can get into that awkward spot.'

'I know.' She made a rueful grimace. 'She talked of going

abroad over Christmas. Not as if she'd booked a holiday, just that she intended going somewhere that's warmer; and she'd a bag half packed.'

Bone thought; *had* she!

A whistle blew long in the playground and after a last rush of feet and some breathless cheerful voices, there was quiet outside.

'Did you see anything else that was, say, out of place or in any way odd?'

'Not a thing. I left her my number in case I could be any help, but I don't think she will call me.'

'I'd better go and see if she'll tell me what's the matter.' Bone put down his mug. 'Thank you for telling me, and for the coffee.'

A rush of feet, and simultaneously with the sound of the bell, the door burst open. Three-T in games kit poured in, checked on seeing Bone, were thrust onwards by those behind, and formed a log jam. Bone stood up, took his coffee mug to the sink and let Mrs Shaw deal with the influx. They came in, giggling, and sorted themselves among the desks, eying Bone and each other. Two of them, nudging, drew attention to what was written on the board, which because of a male presence became suddenly rude. At least, he thought, the previous class had been studying elimination, not reproduction.

He gravely said, 'Goodbye, Mrs Shaw,' She said, 'Goodbye, Mr Bone,' and he left.

She thought, at least it's the end of term. By next term, they'll have got over writing *Mrs Shaw fucks the fuzz* on their rough books, or at best *Grizzle 4 Bone*.

She hoped she had done the right thing by Mrs Lambert. Ought she to have told Miss Mallett instead? Well, it was done. She would give her account to Miss Mallett at lunchtime. Meanwhile, here was Three-T, and she blessed her own forethought as she dealt out banda'd quiz sheets. It was something for them to get on with, and it was all they were capable of at this point of the term, while she went over the conversation with him in her mind.

The patrol car answering a 'Domestic' stopped, blocking the road. There was the aftermath of quite a row. As if mown by a scythe, two men and a woman adorned the small derelict front garden, attended by two women. On the dividing wall sat an elderly man, supported from behind by an elderly lady. His face, alarmingly congested, was the nearest to a codfish in expression that Sergeant Harrison ever wanted to see.

On all fours in the mud near the street fence, a young man was throwing up. He wore only trousers and his back was grazed. Mud clothed him.

A woman sat on the doorstep holding her chest; a blonde girl, supporting her, held a cloth beneath her nose and moved it to and fro.

'All right, then. What's it all about?'

The elderly man and the girl broke out together, trumpet and fife, the elderly lady saying, 'Please, dear,' and clutching her husband's tweed shoulders. The younger policeman helped the youth to his feet and sat him on the windowsill of the bay. Another youth in leathers sat up on the ground. The older policeman, remedying his initial mistake, said to the girl, 'We'll hear you in a minute. Now, sir.'

'Their damned rubbish. Had enough of their slum manners.' He pushed with his toe a yellow wool garment smeared with grease. 'Shoved this in our dustbin.'

The woman on the doorstep said, 'No such thing. I've never seen that before and it's none of ours. Wherever it came from it's not from this house and so I told him.'

'You'd think his bloody dustbin was sacred like the Holy Grail,' the girl said. 'He comes round banging on our door and shouting at Mum, brought on her attack. Bloody bully, calls himself a colonel.'

'I am a colonel—'

'Not in the Army now, are you? Stupid swank, that is. Bloody snob.' She thrust her face at him and the constable edged her back.

'They put their damned rubbish in our dustbin. There was no room left for our own stuff. People of their sort have no business in a neighbourhood like—'

'What's our sort, then?' the youth said, advancing.

'Let's not start anything again, right? No aggro, keep it cool. You don't want trouble. Now, sir, it's Colonel—?'

'Blanchard,' and he gave his regiment.

'You can't want to make a fight over a dustbin, sir. The ladies are upset and this lady's ill.'

'Look,' the girl said, 'I'll tell you. We'd no room in our bin last week and Dad and me put some in the bins on either side. We didn't fill them up, either. Christ, I mean just a few cartons and that, and he takes them all out and throws them on the ground round our bin, like they was doing him some harm or something.'

'It's damned cheek.'

'Maybe we should've asked you, like come round saying "Please Colonel may we have the honour of using your holy dustbin?" But anyway that was last week, and we didn't put that bloody thing in his bin. We've got manners if he hasn't. He said he didn't like it and we didn't do it again. That's not ours.'

'Now, Colonel, look, it's cold out here. Why don't you go indoors with your good lady and have a cup of tea? You heard the young lady say they didn't touch your bin.'

'Who did, then? Who else would put this horrible object in it?' and he picked up the yellow bundle and thrust it at them.

The boy, rubbing his midriff, said, 'Not us. Stand on that.'

'Yellow's not my colour,' the woman said. 'Get inside, Keith, you'll catch your death. You hit my boy, Colonel. I can have you up for that and don't you forget it.'

'You don't want to talk like that,' said the sergeant. 'That's no way for neighbours to talk. It was a mistake. Miss, you take your mother inside and make her a pot of tea. Live and let live.'

The Colonel sent out a ranging glare that suggested a strong difference of opinion on that. He got off the wall, however, and stepped over it, using his wife's arm for balance. He dumped the yellow garment on the wall and plodded to his door. The bundle undid itself and unrolled either side of the wall. They stared.

'That's a bit off,' said the constable. 'Go and ask them if they're sure they've never seen it before. We'd better take it in.'

'I don't want to start them up.'

'Be nice about it. Tactful. In with you.' The sergeant bundled the dress with its startling bloodstains and went to the car. He put the dress in a bag in the boot, moved the car up the road to an empty parking place, and went back to have a word with the neighbour across the road who had reported the disturbance. His colleague emerged from the Pattersons' house shaking his head. They did not ask Mrs Blanchard about the frock. It clearly belonged to a tall woman, and she was barely five foot three.

'No wonder someone wanted rid of that dress,' Harrison said as they drove off.

'It looks like someone had cut their throat down it.'

'That'll do, boy.'

If only they would let him rest! He had been so tired, so cold, hardly able to go on, but they had told him he must find her before she did him any more harm. Always, when he was a little boy, she had said she would kill him one day. He could remember her eyes, fixed on him, her red hair on end, 'the burning fiery bush'. He was always reading about her, even in the Bible. The Bible knew all about murderers and witches. Thou shalt not suffer a witch to live. It was his duty. Whether he was cold or not, however hungry and tired he became, the search would have to go on.

Sometimes he thought he saw the car, and would run after it, but her spells would work and the car would vanish. People hooted and swore at him and she had sent a policeman to talk to him but he had known how to handle that. He wasn't wearing a tie, and the police never like that, so he had held the collar of his coat together against the wind, and put on his most educated voice, talked exactly the way old Doctor Manners did, leaning on his words as though he were surprised at their getting in his way. The policeman had been very polite and only asked him if everything was all right. 'Perfectly, perfectly,' he had said, and made some remark about the weather. They had told him to do that, and it was true that it made people think they needn't worry about you if you could talk about the weather. He had noticed it before, talking to doctors. They relaxed and treated you differently. So he said he was afraid they could expect snow, and the policeman had made some remark about Christmas and wished him a good evening.

Now, suddenly, here was the car. He could remember it very distinctly, cars had once been things he knew a lot about. Somewhere, when they let him, he still knew about them. It was a Ford

Escort, a sand colour, and he recognised the number-plate at once. He touched the top of it in his triumph, the surface was cold and his hands met a surface of greasy dust on the paint; then, because a woman carrying shopping bags was walking towards him on the pavement and looking suspicious he bent to look at one of the tyres as though the pressure might be low. He heard her footsteps go by and straightened himself, smiling. It was so easy to deceive people. Everything was going to be easy, now that he had found the car.

Which was her house, then? They hadn't told him that. Some things he still had to do for himself. The car wasn't outside a house. This was a small side street with gardens backing onto it. He would have to go by the feel. He would be a Hound of the Baskervilles. He would scent her out.

He hesitated by the garden wall facing the car. It wasn't high and he could see over it. There were bushes rustling in the cold breeze, a young maple tree, stick-like hydrangeas waiting for spring to bud. Nothing spoke of Barbara, but then he looked again at the hydrangeas. Mother had always wanted things to look neat in the garden, everything had been clipped and pruned, tied up and kept down. She had hated the look of dead flowers. Mother wanted, like everybody else in this road, to cut off faded flower heads, paper ghosts of what they had been, and Barbara had fought to keep them on, saying they protected buds against the frosts. In this garden alone, the hydrangeas had all the dead brown flowers. He tried the gate.

For some time after Grizel Shaw had left her, she couldn't get rid of the feeling of horror that had come over her when the kitchen door had been opened so wide. It was even difficult for her to get up and shut it, for that meant crossing the gap it made into the room beyond and the sightline from the pane in the garden door. She managed it in the end and it was like closing up a wound. When she sat down again she found she was sweating, and took off the dressing gown she had hurried into when she saw Grizel Shaw from the window. It was a pity that she had been forced to open the door, but she did open it, being afraid of making anyone pay attention to the house, even to the fact that someone evidently could get no answer to the bell. Grizel Shaw would have thought her too ill to get up, perhaps, but someone else might have been watching, wondering. She shivered, and tried, again, to work out what was best. She had nearly finished packing, the flight was booked, she could ring for a taxi when the time came, and run down the steps. There was no real reason that things would not be all right.

She had folded the dressing gown and put it aside, tucked her soft slippers together and fitted them into the bag; then she stopped and listened. Was it her heart thudding or were those footsteps coming up the garden stairs? She stayed bent over the bag, unable to move even when the splintering crash came and steps moved into the kitchen.

Over the bag, as she crouched, she saw the kitchen door jerked open again and he stood there, just as she had known he would, bitter cold coming with him. She stayed bent over the bag, unable to move even when she saw the knife in his hand. He said only her name, 'Barbara,' and lunged.

She stepped back, upright, released from immobility in that second, and dodged behind the sofa. She heard him gasp as he struck a cushion on it and the knife slipped. Then he recovered, stood back again, knife poised, watching her. He had got dreadfully thin and there was grey in his hair. His coat had leaves stuck to the collar, even twigs. Where had he been? Had he eaten? She would have looked after him, oh so gladly, once. He moved, holding the knife at shoulder level, looking at her with those eyes. It wasn't her brother behind those eyes, the brother who had taught her to ride a bicycle, helped with her homework, made up absurd rhymes to give her the giggles. Those eyes wanted to see her dead.

The door to the hall was a few steps away on his right, but he could reach it as fast as she could. She feinted to the left. He copied her on the other side of the sofa. They dodged again, in a horrible parody of their childhood game. As he stepped, however, he caught his heel in the flex that trailed from the standard lamp and she seized her chance. Picking up the bag she had been packing, from beside the sofa, she threw it hard at him and ran for the door.

The doorknob slipped in her grasp but she got into the hall as she heard him scrambling to his feet after the fall the bag had given him. She jerked open the hall door, slammed it at her back and ran full tilt down the carpeted stairs to the door; she slammed that too, dashed between the parked cars and over to the opposite pavement. She had to disappear before he saw her. Wildly she glanced back. Her front door was opening. She turned and crammed herself past a man in the act of leaving the chemist's. As he said loudly 'Excuse me, I'm sure,' she was in the shop, before the counter, looking back at the street again. Dimly, through the lettering on the plate glass, she could see him running down the steps, looking up and down the street. Mr Patel was aware someone had come into the shop, but he was busy making up a prescription; he called out to whoever it was to wait for a moment. He was astounded, and thrown off balance both mental and physical when he felt something bump against his knees and, looking down, saw it was not a dog got in from the street, as he had imagined, but a woman on all fours, her head strained up to him, eyes staring under a fuzz of red hair. Her voice came in a hoarse whisper.

'Ring the police! He's mad. He's just tried to kill me!'

Still holding the little plastic pill tray in which he had been counting Mrs Graves' diuretics, Mr Patel glanced over the division that separated him from the shop. A man was standing at the counter looking in his direction. He was very pale, with turned up coat collar, hands in pockets, but composed in appearance, even severe. Of the two, it was the woman at his feet who looked mad. He hesitated, and the man spoke.

'Have you seen my sister? She's escaped from a mental hospital and I'm afraid she's very dangerous. She thinks everyone is trying to kill her.'

The woman at his feet whimpered very softly and shrank against his leg. Although he could not have heard her the man suddenly left the counter and made to enter the dispensary. Protesting and bewildered, Mr Patel waved the tray at him, scattering diuretics some of which hailed on the woman below. She seemed to be trying to crush herself under the shelves. Following his glance downward, the man pounced; the woman screamed, a loud shocking sound.

It was an undignified, extraordinary struggle. Bottles fell,

Mr Patel waved his arms and shouted, the wrestling match went on as he backed away. Then he saw the knife, and grabbed on the ledge behind him for the phone. He dialled 999 with trembling finger, watching the woman twist from under the knife. The man made a muffled grunt as he missed her and dug the knife into the carpet. Someone came into the shop, whistling, just as his call was answered. He gave his name and address— 'There's a man with a knife!' the phone was knocked from his hand as the man dashed past him; it hung, buzzing and quacking, as the man passed the staring customer and was gone through the glass doors into the street. The woman stayed on her knees amongst the trodden pills, sobbing and holding her head. A pill fell out of her hair as he reached to pick up the phone again.

Bone arrived at Hazeley's office to find an apologetic secretary. Mr Hazeley was not yet there, and a telephone call had come from Inspector Locker: would he ring the station?

Locker said, 'We have Mrs Lambert here. She has been attacked and she says she has something important to tell you. The attack has a bearing on the case, she says, and she insists that she will speak only to you and that it's urgent. I've put out a call on the attacker.'

Beginning already to feel that his talk to Hazeley was not going to be needed, that this was what they had been waiting for instead, Bone told him, 'I'll be there.' To the secretary he said 'My apologies to Mr Hazeley. Something has come up and I must go.' He was already at the door.

Mrs Lambert attacked. He should have gone there first instead of trying to keep the appointment with Hazeley. He chafed at the traffic lights, at the double-parked lorry with winking lights, unloading, that blocked his road; and he parked so swiftly that his car was askew into Superintendent Dallow's slot and he had to back out and park again. He wished the boring old adages weren't so tiresomely true.

Mrs Lambert, with a cup of tea between her hands and W.P.C. Jones at her side, looked across the room at him with fixed wide eyes. Her hair was disarranged, standing out at one side, her brown skirt showed a beige lace slip at the knee, and she had that pallor which on Monday had so struck him. Today's tan sweater failed to warm her colour at all and, once again, she was perspiring.

Bone took off his coat and sat at the side of the desk.

'Now, what happened?'

She put down the cup and said, 'I think I must, I really have to—to tell you everything.'

He put on his receptive face and leant towards her. 'That would be the best thing, Mrs Lambert.'

She gripped her hands together on her knees, the knuckles standing out whitely.

'I don't want to say this. It's dreadful to have to say it. The man. It was my brother. I've been afraid ever since . . .' She put her knuckles to her mouth, gave a sidelong wide glance at Bone and went on, 'He's ill. Mentally ill. He's schizophrenic. I should have told you before but how could I? He's my brother. But he has delusions. He thinks I'm his enemy. He's tried to kill me before. At home.'

'Have you told the police about these previous attacks?'

'No one believes me. He's perfectly able to talk to people and to seem calm and sensible. He is sensible, but it seems to him absolutely sensible that I'm his enemy and have to be killed. He's been in hospital. No one knows what it's like. He killed Claire thinking she was me. You see she had the red wig and my red shawl that he knew.'

'Your shawl?' He remembered the name-tape: Barbara Blake. She was Barbara Lambert now.

'Yes. It was mother's. It's wool challis and very old. I've worked out how it seemed to him. He took poor Claire for me. Someone was seen wandering in the playground, weren't they? It must have been Jonathan. He must have seen her through the window and mistaken her for me. Oh!' She threw her clasped hands down on her lap. 'I've been afraid for so long that he'd find me. I left home, you see, to get away.'

'You say he's been in hospital. They discharged him, did they?'

'Oh yes, they discharged him,' she said bitterly. 'They sent him out as they always did, into community care. Do you know who the community is?' she demanded, whirling round;

'it's me. Me!' and she struck her chest a resounding blow. He thought, there's a lot of violence there.

'What about the social—'

'Oh yes indeed. His social worker came round now and then; a very busy woman, with a large case-load. His social worker, and that's exactly what it meant. Not mine! Jonathan could terrorise me, and if I complained, then I was uncaring. Uncaring. I dare say she had read up schizophrenia in the books but she didn't know schizophrenics. Don't think me heartless. I know he was suffering. He does suffer. But she thought that I simply didn't want the trouble of looking after him. Trouble! Looking after him! Good God, he wouldn't let me leave the house! I told her. I told her what he was like. Sitting staring with a knife in his hand. He carried a knife all the time. He had one today.'

Bone fleetingly wondered what had become of this knife. That the murderer had used one from the D.S. drawer.

'He wouldn't let me go out in case I communicated with his enemies. I told her. And do you know, he would talk to her so rationally. He told her he knew he was unreasonable with me and just wished I would understand. He wouldn't eat in my presence. He would sit watching me eat and then take his plate to his room, and keep coming out to see what I was doing. He wouldn't let me into his room even to change the sheets or take the plates away. Do you know what she said to me? She said she knew it was difficult. *She* knew it was difficult! And I must be understanding. I said to her, do you know what I have to understand? He sits there all day, all evening. With a knife in his hand. He thinks I am his enemy. And she said, "Perhaps you are his enemy. You want him back in hospital, don't you? Your own brother?" and I said, "I'm his own sister, but he doesn't care about that." "But's he's ill," she said, "and you're not." "I shall be, if it goes on" I said. So she said, "He's all right, you know. There's no danger while he's taking the medication." And I said, "He isn't, he won't take it. He tells you he is, but he isn't. How am I supposed to cope with it? What am I to do?" and she said, "He needs you. He needs your loving understanding."'

She sat hunched now, trembling. Bone said, feeling the inadequacy of the words, 'I'm sorry.'

'I left there. I left my home. He started wandering the roads at night and he made a mistake, he frightened somone else as well as me and they took him back into hospital. So while he was gone, I left. I changed my name, took a married name. I'm not married. I said I was divorced. Oddly enough people don't check on that. My testimonials were in my own name, but only Miss Mallett and Miss Cantrell knew what that was. I left a *Poste Restante* address. I go there to collect letters once a week. There hardly are any. But they wrote from hospital to say they were discharging him. I don't know why. The time before that he simply arrived. Perhaps the fuss I made then got them to give warning this time. Well, I wrote back, and sent my letter to a friend in Wales to post for me, saying I was not able to help. But somehow they still seem to have let him go. There was the house he could live in, I suppose. Or they forgot to pass my letter to the right person. He traced me. I suppose the Post Office told him the town of the *Poste Restante*. I saw him in the street outside the school on Monday morning. Then yesterday he came suddenly and beat on my car when I was driving down Mount Pleasant. I was appalled! So afraid. And if he had killed her, you could almost say I was responsible,' and she gave a little sick smile. 'I didn't tell you. I should have done. But I was so—he's my brother. But all the same he's got to be found and stopped. He can't tell his imaginings from what's real. It's some barrier normal people have that he hasn't got.'

'Of course you had to tell us. We'll find him, Mrs Lambert.'

'Miss Blake,' she said. 'I'm Barbara Blake. Oh, find him, find him. I need to be safe, you see. Please, is there some place where I can stay to be safe?'

Mrs Lawrence had waited until six to telephone Edward, and she was satisfied with what they had agreed. Edward had dismissed her doubts as to who owned Claire's little house. It had of course to be either her or Dadda; and as he was in Australia she could act on his behalf. It was necessary to get that dreadful, that disgusting couple out of the basement, and they should be given notice quickly, in all fairness. She therefore put on her coat and hat and left the hotel to walk there straight away.

The streets were dry now at least, the sky still overcast but the wind had dropped. Only a chill breeze turned the corner of her coat back, at the corner into the main street. She reflected that the town had a different feeling from last time, when she had been staying with Claire. She felt more of a stranger, rootless without Claire's presence. The town had an emptiness. It was no longer Claire's home.

She had quite a walk across the town to the quiet side street. She had been looking up property prices and had been happily surprised to see what she might expect to get for this really very modest little house.

She glanced at the façade as she headed for the basement steps, and she stopped in her tracks. There was a light showing and the front door was ajar. Someone was in Claire's house, her house.

That could not be right. If it was the police, they should not leave the front door open. If it was those creatures from downstairs, they were due for a piece of her mind.

She ran up the steps and in, oblivious to the raw wood round the door lock.

Downstairs Teddy, in a chef's apron printed with 'I'm the hottest thing in the kitchen,' dished up the chops, put the gravy jug next to Merc's plate, and dealt potatoes from the pan. The sprouts were just done in time. He checked that everything was there, and sat down. Merc had started. He had such a good appetite, it was really worthwhile cooking for someone so appreciative.

'What was that noise?'

Merc, chewing, raised his head. A car went by the house and Teddy shrugged. 'Must have been mistaken. Or it was the local paper. The boy always makes a clatter getting it through the box. Claire used to—'

He stopped.

'That's footsteps. Oh, it must be the police. Do you suppose it's the dreamboat or just the Inspector?'

Merc was not interested, so Teddy fell silent and cut up his chop. It *was* nicely cooked. Merc passed the gravy.

Both men suspended eating. There had been a cry from overhead.

'Did someone call "Claire"? Was it "Claire"?'

They listened, Merc's jaws moving at a slower rate.

'Isn't that a bit . . . Is it someone who shouldn't be there?'

Merc was not long distracted from the meal, and, as he indicated with an economical grimace, they couldn't do much if there were an intruder. Teddy hesitated with his eye on the phone. 'Shouldn't we do something?'

Quick steps sounded overhead, light, a woman's. A voice called out. Teddy put down his fork. 'I'd have sworn that was Claire. Didn't it sound like her voice? Of course I'm imagining.'

Feet came down the stairs in the house above. A moment later, a woman's voice screamed and screamed.

Merc downed tools and was up the basement stairs like a panther. Teddy said, 'Oh my God don't. That's a maniac. Don't.' He saw Merc, his back against the wall in the half-dark, jack-knife one leg and drive his foot at the lock of the door. Teddy dived for the phone.

Merc came through the door into a shower of earth, leaves and broken china. A man had come down the stairs and now, one arm up to protect his head, and an odd-shaped weapon in the other hand, he advanced on the screaming woman while she seized Claire's plants from the shelves and tables and hurled them. She was a terrible shot, but the missiles were like shells, bursting on wall and ceiling so that a shrapnel of stems and leaves, of shards and soil, flew in from unlooked-for sources. Merc ducked and went for the man in a crouching run. The man propelled a heavy armchair into his path. The woman, maintaining on every breath a long shrill note like a demented steam-whistle, ran out of plants and threw a vase that hit the ceiling light. In the resultant dark, the man showed up in front of the window heading for the street door. Merc dived.

He almost got him. They both met a small table by the window which became firewood. The brass vase full of dead chrysanthemums fell and the man yowped. Merc, slithering in wet flowers, got to his feet in the hall doorway and the man wavered. The headlights of a passing car showed a standard lamp charging across the room at him, aimed like a battering ram by the galloping woman.

He headed for the kitchen. Teddy erupted in his path with the heavy frying pan. He turned and grappled with the standard lamp, pulling its shade awry and trying to wrest the shaft from the woman. One hand closed on the shaft and switched the light on. Blinded, she staggered back and let go, and he flailed the base of the lamp round in the direction of Merc. It would have been a good move had Merc been where he thought, but Merc, having run up five treads of the staircase and vaulted the banisters, was coming in just below ceiling height. The man dropped the lamp and snatched from his belt the weapon he had held before, but Merc's foot got him in the soft upper arm. The two men crumpled into a heaving tangle on the floor. Shadows from the rolling lamp made nonsense of whatever was happening down there. Teddy danced above it with the pan raised. He struck once as the man's rump rose for a second, but he struck no more. There was a convulsion and Merc came out on top, kneeling astride, with the man face down, his wrists up between his shoulder-blades in Merc's grasp. There was a silence full of whistling breath.

Bone, brought onto the scene by an alert desk sergeant thirteen minutes later, came through the broken door to, apparently, a nasty accident in a greenhouse. A standard lamp with no shade, and a wall sconce, shone on scattered loam, leaves and broken pots on every surface.

Merc rose, always further than one expected, from one of the Jacobean chairs. He indicated a trussed figure on the floor. Teddy pattered up from downstairs and said 'Oh!' sharply on seeing Bone. The uniform branch, Sergeant Harrison and young Smith, took up the man from the floor, who gazed about but said nothing. The red hair, and a fleeting likeness to Mrs Lambert—Miss Blake—told who he was, but Bone asked him. He broke out into prophetic utterances, however, events having shaken him out of coherence. Bone gave directions about doctors and, when they had gone, examined the front door and its splintered wood.

'That will have to be nailed up.'

'Merc can do it,' Teddy said. 'It's freezing here. Come downstairs.'

Merc picked up a wooden chest and rammed it between the door and the arch-foot just inside, wedging in a dictionary to assure a good fit for the extempore closure. 'There!' Teddy could not resist a little showmanship on Merc's behalf. He went on, 'We've got Mrs Lawrence downstairs,' as if offering a particular enticement, 'and coffee. And more if you're allowed it.'

Teddy showed him where Merc had burst the lock of the basement stairs, and Bone went with them past the decorated plates. In the warm and lighted basement, Aimée Lawrence sat on the sofa-bed with a glass in her hand. Teddy pulled forward an armchair and said to her, 'Do you know Detective-Superintendent Bone?'

'Aye,' she said, 'We've met.'

Teddy sat down beside her and, to Bone's amazement, took her hand. 'Mrs Lawrence has had *the* most terrifying time,' he said. A brandy bottle stood foursquare next to the coffeepot on the table among abandoned plates with pan lids on them preserving the food.

'I came by the house,' she said, 'and what should I see but the door open, and lights on.' Her blue-grey eyes found Bone for a moment and lost him. He thought, She's tight. 'Of course I came in, and I called out who was there, and who should appear but a maniac? A maniac. He'd a great knife in his hand.'

Teddy leant forward and said confidentially, 'It was a cold chisel.' She paid little attention to this, except to tap the hand that held hers with the foot of her glass.

'He attacked me. Or,' a sudden caution and native love of truth striking through, 'I thought he would. I kept him off.'

'She threw the plants at him,' said Teddy admiringly.

Bone accepted a mug of coffee surprisingly offered him by Merc. He was tired, dazed after the volubility of Barbara Blake. Something about the coffee, which he gratefully swallowed, made him stop, sniff at it and look at Merc; who sat astride a chair watching Aimée. Bone went on drinking the coffee, reckless for once.

146

'They saved my life,' she said. 'Merc arrived on the scene in the nick of time. And Teddy!' The glass, raised to them with the hand of inebriation, spun a drop out onto Teddy's thigh. He brushed it off with the backs of his fingers, and stared at her with a certain pride, as if he had invented her.

'I don't know what would have happened without them.' She in her turn now leant forward confidentially to Bone. 'They're old friends of Claire's, you know. They've tellt me how she would come down and sit here.'

Teddy wiped a rapid finger under his eye, but maintained his social smile. He may be lit, Bone thought, but he liked Claire Fairlie. He minds that she's dead. Not many people do. His thoughts took a brief march around the people who would mind if he himself died; revolted at this sentimentality, he brought himself swiftly back to the matter in hand.

'He broke in, then.'

'Wasn't it fantastic? I thought at first it might be you, Mr Bone, but I wasn't quite easy, was I, Merc? And I thought he called out "Claire". Could he have done?'

'He must have met her,' Aimée said, 'else why would he come here? A home-icidal mair-niac.'

'You may have had a very lucky escape, Mrs Lawrence.'

'Luck had not the slightest thing to do wi'it. These gentlemen saved my life. They came to my rescue at risk to themselves.' She leant forward again, got Bone into focus and said to him in measured tones, 'I ... was ... a ... daid ... woman.' Leaning back, she said, 'As she was,' and drained her glass.

Bone said, 'Let me run over the facts. You,' to Teddy, 'heard a noise overhead.'

'No, first a noise at the door. I thought it was the local paper. The boy makes such a clatter. Claire used to say how careful he was never to leave the paper in the letter-box, he always pushed it right through. It must have been the door being forced, though. With that dirty great chisel. God, when Merc jumped him and I saw that chisel pointed right at him— but I should have known Merc would cope.'

Merc, impassive, had nevertheless a swollen cheekbone.

'But that was later. We thought, after we heard him come

in, that he called out "Claire", and I was in five minds about getting in touch with you then.'

He and Aimée told the story. Bone, all the better for the fierce slug of brandy in his coffee, let them put it together for him. Jonathan Blake had found a bizarre reception committee when he came looking for Claire. Did he know he had killed her? What had brought him to this house? Something was odd about that, but Bone felt decidedly more cheerful about sorting it out than he had done.

'That's not the first door he's forced,' he said as he rose. 'It's a speciality of his.'

Before he left, he supervised Merc's nailing up of the front door; then everyone went out by the basement. Merc and Teddy were escorting Aimée to her hotel.

As he slid behind the wheel of his car, Bone remembered that it was a temperance hotel.

He himself drove with care.

CHAPTER
12

It seemed a long time before he could get home. Mrs Lambert, who had gone out to Adlingsden to stay the night with Mrs Shaw, was quite euphoric at her brother's capture. She spoke of going on holiday with an easy mind. She knew, she said, it sounded callous but Mr Bone understood the situation.

Mr Bone asked her if she intended going abroad.

Yes, straight after school broke up tomorrow. It was all booked and she could finish packing in no time.

Mr Bone had to ask her, regretfully, to postpone leaving the country. Her evidence about her brother's involvement with the death was still necessary, and she must in any case attend the magistrates' court for his committal for breaking and entering and for his attack on her. Yes, it was a pity. He hoped the airline would be able to accommodate her later; and the hotel; he was sorry.

Well then, of course, yes. She would have to stay.

Bone rang off. They could hold Blake for that, but the evidence connecting him with Claire Fairlie's death was tenuous indeed. He had gone to her house; why? It was the only thing that connected him with her. It suggested that he had known her. He had possibly called her name, as if he expected her to be alive. Had he killed her thinking she was his sister, and not recognised her after death? She had been stabbed from behind. The wig, Bone thought, was not so like Barbara Blake's hair, but who could tell how it seemed, might have seemed, to a man whose perceptions were abnormal?

Until he lost it at the chemist's, Blake had carried a knife. Why use a D.S. one?

And the murderer must have been splashed with blood. Blake would not say where his clothes were or where he had been living, so as yet any evidence on that was missing too. A search of the lockups, outhouses and derelict buildings was going on, to find where he might have been, or to find stained clothing. Bone did not yet feel a sense of accomplishment or of relief, that he had got a case solved, that a dangerous man, a killer, was no longer at large.

For one thing, he had no feeling that he had brought this about. The whole case, complicated right from the start by a number of suspects superfluous to requirements, had continued of its own momentum, boosted by fortuitous happenings, and he had been dragged in the slipstream. There had been times, during the last few nights, when his mind had felt like a hamster in a wheel, pattering round fast to no profit. Each day had brought either a couple of fresh suspects or a further freak-show like yesterday's attack on Mrs Lambert—Miss Blake—and the capture of Jonathan Blake by Merc of all people. It had seemed Bone's part to be auditor but not actor in these scenes. Still, he should be satisfied.

He could not expect explanation from Jonathan Blake, veering in his talk from rationality to the fantastic without any change of face or bearing, his only sign of disturbance the serious assertion that he must do as he was told, which was why 'I kill my sister.' Not 'killed', but 'kill', as if it were a continual process. Bone was edgy with the unease of it. Yet the Chief had been complimentary.

In the morning he dropped Charlotte off at the school that now looked familiar, a place he had worked in. She scuttled through the rain. He saw a figure with a black shock of hair go alongside her, take Cha's schoolbag from her shoulder and hitch it onto her own, and Beverly loped beside Charlotte talking to her. Another source of unease, for Beverly's kindness was a doubtful quantity.

In his own office he sat in front of the files of work in hand, grimaced at them and re-arranged them all, precisely aligning the base of the telephone with the edge of the blotter and rectangularising everything. When he saw what he was doing, it seemed to him an expression of his sense of chaos.

It must be Christmas; he never liked Christmas, not since Petra died, anyway. Last year he'd been on duty and glad of it, until he realised that Cha, instead of having a good time at Alison's with her cousins, had been bored, tongue-tied and dismayed. His own childhood Christmases had been an embarrassment of over-eating, over-excitement, boozy uncles, bossy Alison. Whatever he arranged this year with Cha would fall short of what Petra would have done. Yet he did look forward to it in a way. Dante spoke of the dread, the rejection, of steep stairs in other people's houses: Bone could vouch for the cheerlessness of other people's roast turkey.

Today's work stared at him and he resolutely started in on the dreary paperwork. Then the door opened with a brief accompanying knock and Locker walked in.

'Hallo. Want a week off for shopping, Steve?'

'That'll be the day. Good work last night, sir, getting hold of Jonathan Blake.'

'The good work was courtesy of Merc Quinn; a man of action rather than words.'

'I was talking to Blake this morning while we were waiting at the court. He asked me to get in touch with Claire Fairlie, who could help him; he said she promised to help him. He doesn't recollect being at her house last night.'

'She promised to help him? That's the connection, then. Where did they meet? Could he tell you?'

'He was asking at the schools for his sister,' Locker said. 'Of course he didn't know she was using the name of Lambert, so no joy, but in her usual manner of helping lame ducks to the nearest pond Fairlie offered to help.'

'If he doesn't remember last night, he could have attacked Claire without remembering it. I'm not too happy with this theory of the wandering maniac—how are we getting on with the search for clothes?'

'Nothing on men's clothes. Harrison and Smith were at a barney in Parloe Road yesterday, some feudin' and fussin' over a dustbin, and they got a dress with some blood on it. Said it looked like a bad nosebleed, or it might belong to a woman who'd picked up a run-over dog in Hart Lane on Sunday night.'

Bone got up. 'Let's go have a look-see.'

The plastic bag held a yellow dress. What was it about a yellow dress? It stirred in the landscape before Bone's inner eye but would not come into view. They manoeuvred the bag, trying to see the extent of the stain. It seemed comprehensive.

'Steve,' said Bone, as the cloth altered colour under the light, '*what* was Mrs Lambert wearing on Monday night?'

Locker bent to look. 'I think it was something that colour all right. I think it was.'

'Any case there was against Jonathan Blake rests on her.' He wanted to take the dress out to make sure, but knew better. The lab would have trouble enough with dustbin traces, without bits of his own hair and the station's dust.

'Get it to the lab, Steve. Urgent, for matching with Fairlie's. May have Fairlie's hair and Lambert's. She was wearing a sweater over it, in Miss Mallett's hothouse. Remember how she sweated and said she felt cold? Wish I could get hold of that sweater. It could be somewhere in the school or in her flat. Or she threw it away separately; it must have blood on the inside.'

If the traces on the dress could prove it Lambert's, with Fairlie's blood, although motive was unclear, she might be the one. Blake could well be telling the truth, that he had gone to Claire Fairlie's house expecting to find her, and desperate enough to break in when she did not answer. Blake had come to Tunbridge Wells in search of his sister, a teacher. He had met, by asking at school gates, a teacher who loved to help, but who knew no Barbara Blake . . .

He said to the already absent Steve, 'We may be onto it.'

Suddenly he picked up the phone. It was unreasonable, foolish, but he had to know. Miss Cantrell answered, 'Haddon House School. Yes, Mrs Lambert and Mrs Shaw are both in this morning. Mrs Lambert is much better.'

Bone thanked her. He thought how ridiculous it was. Yet if Lambert, and he was saying Lambert to himself now as if she were already under arrest, if she were a murderer he disliked to think of her near Grizel Shaw. Blithe, he thought, wasn't that a Scots word? It was Grizel Shaw.

He looked at his watch. Cha's carol concert was at eleven. She had hoped he could go. At breakfast she'd looked pale. These two terms had been difficult. The school, although she liked it, held so much to get used to, faces, customs, attitudes, ways of teaching. She had, it turned out, quite liked Claire Fairlie, who had been kind to her. It was Cha's sagacity, her experience as a disabled child, that made her distrust the particular sympathy she was given. She preferred Miss Dunne, who gave no sympathy, only matter-of-fact patience. He would be at her carol concert. He could just make it.

He arrived early. Someone was practising on the Hall piano, a phrase over and over, dashing notes in the air. The entrance hall made a passage for girls carrying chairs, piles of books, two with armfuls of clothing. These last stopped wearily.

'Is there anywhere we *haven't* been?'

'No, but with people messing about we could've missed some.'

'You mean we've got to cart this stinking lot round again?'

'No. If they've missed it, that's their rotten luck. We'll dump the lot back on Mrs Tudor. She can—Oh, sorry.'

She had seen Bone, and they stood aside for him cheerfully.

'Lost property still?'

'Do you want any?'

'Unless you've got my daughter's sweater. I don't think any of the rest would fit me.'

'Sweaters?' They sifted through their armfuls, but found no sweater of any size. It would have been too much to expect. They bore their burdens away to Mrs Tudor, and a flood of seniors came down the stairs and headed for the Hall. Among the last, Cha negotiated the stairs with Grue idling beside her.

'Hallo.'

'We can't keep meeting like this,' Grue said, and followed the rest into Hall.

'I shall miss seeing you round school next term,' Cha said. She had put all her hair up on top since this morning. Perhaps it had needed Grue's help to achieve. The shape of her head, with the shining knot on top, was fragile, young.

'Like the hair,' he said seriously.

'Good.'

He nodded and they parted.

In the Hall children were bringing chairs and lining them up. Paper chains hung on the walls, and over the portraits of past headmistresses holly was stuck—but not mistletoe, Bone noted. The plastic mistletoe hung from a light fitting under the gallery, almost over the head of Miss Dare, who in a track-suit was vigorously directing the chair-carriers.

There was a festive freedom about people's movements and voices, not like the tension before the opera. The piano-player had stopped now. Someone began to strum 'Chopsticks' and was told off.

Some more parents had arrived, mainly women at this time of day. A bell rang, scattering the girls out of sight and leaving only the prefects, some with a pile each of song sheets, at the doors, others, ushering parents to places, trying to get them not to take aisle seats but to move to the centre. Bone took a song sheet from Tabitha St John and stood about, wanting an aisle place. After about fifteen minutes of waiting, reading his carols and greeting Martin and Nicola Grant and other relations of pupils whom he knew, he took a seat.

Almost at once, a masterful hand struck chords on the piano, the voices died to a hush, and on the far side of the Hall a solo voice, coolly pure, began.

> *Adeste, fideles,*
> *Laete triumphante,*
> *Adeste, adeste,*
> *In Bethlehem.*

The audience surged or floundered to its feet and he could not see who the soloist was, but the Latin processed up the far side of the Hall, solo, chorus, descant, solo, until reaching the stage they filed up and flung the final *Venite adoremus!* to the roof in full voice.

Throughout the concert, whether he sat listening or stood and sang, Bone was conscious of the exhilaration in the Hall, of excitement that no doubt sprang partly from gruesome memories of the last entertainment there only a few days ago, partly and mainly from anticipation of holidays, of Christmas. Two thousand years of celebrating peace on earth, and the police were still arresting murderers. An old charwoman who had helped his mother once when she was ill had a favourite repeated comment on life: 'There's none so deaf as those that won't hear.' People got on with their lives, taking notice of the Christmas message about as much as they did of the amplifiers blaring out carols on the street, and objecting if it got too intrusive.

Christmas was a time when people were forced into proximity with those whom they successfully avoided the rest of the year. Drink relaxed their inhibitions. The family, that pressure-cooker of emotion, was set to blow ... It was a time, perhaps, when people saw what mostly they tried not to see, the gap between what they believed they should feel and what in fact they felt.

Everybody stood now for the final processional, and Bone rose with them, keeping his eyes on Mrs Lambert's red head conspicuous in the middle of the front row, next to Miss Mallett's greying French pleat. Here was the cat, there the mouse. Perhaps cats were not cruel at all; they were just waiting for the invisible policewoman to arrive so that they could pounce. Was this, after it all, really the right mouse?

Claire Fairlie had attracted people to her by virtue of her good intentions. Nothing so deadly as good intentions badly received. One could not force good intentions on others. Bone had a very good idea of what he might be about to hear from Mrs Lambert's lips, and he was no less sorry for her on that account.

The choir was going past, led by Sarah Crouch, trying to keep their eyes on the doors and not let them stray to seek parents' faces. Charlotte came, her topknot shining as she paced beside Grue, keeping her steps as level as she could, keeping her eyes steadily ahead, as careful of their custody as any nun. Bone reflected on the discipline she showed, the strength of character that had emerged since the accident, and that made him so proud of her. Would his little son have grown up so brave?

He crumpled the carol sheet and fixed his own eyes determinedly, as was his duty, on the red head now slowly approaching behind Miss Mallett. By keeping the procession and the carol going, the staff reached the entrance hall while the parents had to stay in their seats. Then, however, Bone slid out.

Miss Mallett halted him to deliver a dignified compliment on his handling of the 'horrible episode'. What a good choice of word, placing the nastiness of Fairlie's death on its temporal plane, firmly disinfecting it within the boundaries of last Monday. Bone might, in the nature of things, go on to other such episodes. Miss Mallett clearly felt she had had her ration in this life.

Beyond her, Mrs Lambert, talking to parents, had neared the main doors, and Bone now made his way swiftly between shoulder and backs towards her. At the top of the entrance steps, P.C. Fredricks stood, giving her imitation of a watchful horse. He touched Mrs Lambert's sleeve to get her attention in the crowd and, when she turned, felt sorry at her smile. Of course, he was the rescuer, the remover of her fear.

'Can you come now?'

'Of course. I'm supposed to be at the Christmas staff lunch —will it take long?'

'I can't say.'

'Jon's safe?' Fear widened her eyes as instantly as her face blanched.

'Yes, he's quite safe.'

'Happy Christmas, Mrs Lambert. Thanks for everything! Have a lovely holiday.' Julia Craven thrust an envelope, through which showed the bright colours of a card, into Mrs Lambert's passive hand, smiled at them both and rushed off. Fredricks now stood close behind Mrs Lambert but no one stopped to stare. The presence of police in the school, though perhaps an unpleasant reminder, had come to be accepted. Bone's casual air precluded emotion.

She walked down the steps, got into the car, saying nothing. He could not tell whether she thought anything was wrong. All that troubled her seemed to be that her brother should stay safely in his cell. In the car, they were silent, though she turned to him once or twice. He wore his absent, preoccupied face and said nothing. It was in the station, in his office, that the cat pounced.

'You were wearing a yellow dress on Monday, Miss Blake. What did you do with it?'

She clasped her hands and stood silent for a moment. 'I spilt something on it. Sauce. I threw it away.'

'In a dustbin at the back of Parloe Road, by any chance?'

'I don't know where.' She brought the knuckles of her hands to her mouth. 'You can't have found it.'

'Why not put it in your own dustbin?'

She said nothing for a minute, then, 'You've got to understand that it was Jonathan.'

He thought she was about to repeat her accusations of her brother, and drew breath, but she went on, 'Claire met him.'

'Barbara Blake,' he interrupted; for he must not let her say more until he had spoken. 'You are under arrest for the murder of Claire Fairlie. You do not have to say anything unless you wish to do, but what you say may be given in evidence.'

'Yes. Yes. I know. I took my shawl in, you see, that Mairi had been going to wear for the part, and she shook it out and she caught up the corner and said, "*You're* Barbara Blake. Of course you are. Barbara Lambert, Barbara Blake. Do you know your brother is looking for you?"'

She bent suddenly, her hands between her knees. Fredricks came forward and put a chair for her, made her sit down.

'As if I didn't know!' She looked up at Bone, and spoke with exasperation. 'As if I hadn't been keeping out of his way ever since I saw him, and dreading he'd find me. I'd thought it was him that morning, I'd hidden behind my car. I pretended to have dropped something, in case anyone had seen me. *He* didn't, which was all that mattered. It doesn't matter now, though. Isn't that strange? But you want to know about Claire. She said "Jon will be so glad I've found you," and I thought, Jon indeed. But I said "You're not to tell him." I said, "You don't understand about him. He's told you lies, he always does. I haven't come all this way and started a new life away from him to be dragged through all that horror again. You don't know what he's like. No one does." Oh, I don't know what I said. I've gone over it again so often that I don't know what I did say. I've put arguments she'd have had to listen to, but she wouldn't listen. She sat there, making up her eyelashes and talking to the mirror, not listening, talking about my duty and his need, not talking to me, but as if she was saying it all for her own satisfaction. He was the afflicted one and he needed care and love. I only had to love him, she said. It was my rejection he couldn't stand, my rejection that made him behave in a way he knew I didn't like. I must love him. She looked at me then and gave me that stupid smile and said yes, she would tell him, because of his need, and because she knew I really did need someone to care for. She said, "It's easy if you think of other people, if you have love." She think of other people! She who kept poor Ian Sharpe on a string suffering. She who dropped people she got tired of, even the children who didn't know what they'd done. And there was the drawer with "knives" marked on it. I thought of Jonathan knowing where I was, and being there sitting with his knife staring, of all I'd gone through, and there was she making up her face to sing Beverly Braun's part and prating about love. I'm really not quite sure what I did,' and here she glanced apologetically at Bone, 'but I pulled the shawl away. She shouldn't have been making up with it on, but no one ever cares for other people's things. And I struck her. She fell forward and there was quite a lot of blood. You don't think it would do that, you think blood will simply ooze, but there was a little thin jet that got all over me. Then she fell back, and I'd moved a bit away from her somehow. So I wiped the knife's handle and the drawer, and I washed myself, my hands I mean, and I used kitchen tissues on my dress, but of course it was too bad for them to be much use. I didn't know what to do with them, so I put them inside my dress because it felt wet through my clothes. Later on that seemed a very odd thing for me to have done. Then when it was all quiet in the passage, with the girls on stage, I went to my place. I knew there was a jersey lying there, someone had left it on the edge of the stage, and I put it on. It hid everything. I was sure that things would be all right. And they were, too. I heard myself saying all the right things, as if it was someone else, the person who had not done anything. And late at night I went and put the clothes in dustbins, in different bins here and there. Some bins are put out in the back alleys the night before dustmen come, because the men come so early. I meant to push the dress under, but a motorbike was coming round the corner, so I walked away. That was how it was found, I suppose.'

She did not speculate on how it had reached Bone.

'I did kill her,' she said. 'I shall be in prison a long time, shan't I? I'll be safe there. They'll let him out. They always do. But I shan't be around.'

She looked at Bone and actually smiled. He wondered, with an unpleasant chill, if when they finally let her out, she would look around for another passport to her own peculiar kind of freedom.

CHAPTER
13

Martin Grant put work on his A-levels first when there was any helping in the house to be done before Christmas. He declared the season to be an outworn expression of a pagan belief co-opted by early Christians, and he stated that since he himself had not invited the homeless couple and their baby to whom his parents were giving hospitality, he saw no need for him to entertain them. When the merrymaking actually started, he was at first morose, but joined in before long, graciously and with the air of one humouring children. His sister had given him, at his request, Machiavelli's *The Prince*, and he read this for some time while the games were going on, but it did not engage his attention. Some of it was even dismayingly hard to follow. Besides, he knew the answers to some of the questions in the game that were stumping the rest, and this proved irresistible. He had been pretty upset about Claire, and knew he would be, off and on, for some time. With a burst of courage, however, that was not negligible, he decided against dramatising his loss. He would join in, and not let anybody know, except perhaps Prue afterwards, that he had suffered.

Harry Birch spent a good part of the season getting glumly drunk, and remaining so. He had formed the intention of getting out and going north again in the New Year, trading once more on the time lag his reputation took to catch up with him. He had to be careful, now this new law was out, of applying only to private schools; he preferred comprehensives because they were usually sizeable and he could be anonymous, but it was no go if he had to declare any form he'd got and the police would be onto him. He spoke darkly against police harassment, with all the outrage of a man who could easily have been guilty if he'd tried.

Mrs Braun liked a family Christmas, but she wondered why. Given her mother and her daughter, gaiety was problematical. Bev said they were the Scots Family MacCabre, and she distributed her skull Christmas cards, but on the day she hugged her mother quite affectionately, gave her a nice bottle of perfume, and settled in front of the telly quietly enough with crisps. She was wearing a tee-shirt with the legend *Fuck the World*. Mrs Braun said it wasn't a seasonable message, but in the interests of harmony she said it mildly. Her mother, who had a strict rule about not drinking anything strong before six o'clock, when she started on the gin, recognised Christmas by starting on it right after breakfast, on the bottle Bev had given her. Brenda had two gentleman friends and a woman from down the street who lived alone, to join them for lunch, and she was in the kitchen, sweating, swearing, swigging and cooking, shouting through to Bev to tell her when someone she liked was on telly. Bev was off after lunch to a basement party, by candlelight, but she was not made up for it yet. The old dear from down the road struck up a real witches' combo with Mrs Staice, and after lunch was raucously singing old songs with her while Brenda dozed between her gentlemen friends on the sofa before the telly, doors shut on the kitchen shambles of wrecked turkey and piles of dishes. The Queen made her speech with the gracious air of someone who has glimpsed the kitchen but is aware that some of us are human.

Sharpe spent the day with his widowed mother who, apart from a lack of quite his quality of moustache, and the possession of spectacles much thicker, strongly resembled him. He was indulgent to her, drinking sherry more sweet than he liked, helping to wheel the hostess trolley from the immaculate kitchen. They had roast goose and red cabbage, her traditional fare. He had two helpings of trifle and sipped his coffee afterwards, reflecting on the blessed absence of children. Somewhere, tenuously, the thought crossed his mind that marriage to Claire Fairlie would not have been so peaceful. It was even difficult for him to imagine how he could have become so caught up in the obsession of the last few months, with its dreadful climax. In some way, which it would be interesting to analyse when he was more detached about it, the appalling moments of holding her body, lifeless in his arms, had purged him ... Who could think that Mrs Lambert, that pleasant woman, could do a thing so terrible? *Die welche Gott verderben will, verblendet Er vorher.*

Beverly, her face a symphony of white, black, purple and silver, went off to her party; it was so dark by the smouldering candles that you couldn't tell who was doing whom, the amps gave out a sound that carried you high. She danced to Ken Cryer's *Screaming down the sky*, and waited for her boyfriend to arrive. She knew he would be late because it would cost him a row with his parents to get out of the house today. She was in no hurry. This party was going to go on for hours.

Teddy and Merc were having another sort of basement party. It was to have been a house-cooling party when Teddy thought they were going to have to leave, but there was now a strong possibility that they would be expanding into the rest of the house as Aimée preferred 'Tenants she knew she could trust.' Teddy had persuaded her that it was foolish to sell property when you could rent it and let the value increase. He meant to use the basement for storing furniture not displayed in the shop, a tremendous advantage. He had popped upstairs for a look round; they had helped Aimée to clear up and he was considering the decor. No use pretending Claire had any visual sense, she preferred *people*, poor darling. He wandered about, alone, glass in hand, touching things, brushing earth out of a corner, looking at pictures. Downstairs the party was thrumming, a comfortable noise of music and voices came up, and the rhythm was palpable through the floor. On impulse he picked up the telephone and dialled long-distance, a number from Claire's pop-up phone pad.

'Am I interrupting your afternoon? I just had to call you, Aimée, to wish you a Happy Christmas, and say we're having a lovely party ... Yes, I look forward to meeting him ... Oh dear, I do hope nothing too dreadful?—*we've* been telling our friends about *you* and how lucky we are ... Very happy, but *goodness* how we do miss Claire, she loved a party. It's like a little pain all the time ... Yes, Merc has started decorating upstairs ... nonsense, it's cheap rate today, but all the same I mustn't keep chattering, you'll have better things to do ... Well, I've rescued a lot of the plants and they look quite healthy, rather proud of themselves for saving your life ...'

When he rang off, he stood looking round a minute. Claire, he thought, such a lovely person. We had such fun, such laughs.

He turned to the basement door, and opened it on the roar of noise, into which he plunged like a strong swimmer into a sea.

Bone and Charlotte had opened presents over breakfast, and the cat Ziggy had received a catmint toy. His interest in it was considerable, but his real joy was losing it in the wrapping paper. Even if it was in plain view, the paper flowered for him with invisible mice on every side. He would crouch low, tail slapping the floor, and spring. He would follow the unseen run of an escaping phantom mouse the other side of a fold of paper, and stun it with an overarm slash at the end. He ran head first into a paper bag and his hind legs went on running as the bag crossed the carpet and fetched up against the wall. He came out shaking his ears, and Charlotte reversed the bag—'But he won't do it again once it hurt his head.' Ziggy perceived that his dire foe still lived in the bag, plunged in, and drove it back across the carpet and under the sofa, his shadow-striped hind legs and tail active on view, his front paws thrashing in the bag. Bone laughed out loud in a releasing shout.

They made the lunch together, Bone cleaning the chicken, Charlotte doing sprouts and potatoes. She did more cooking than he; 'Cooks with L-plates,' she said, but she was at least being taught how to do it, while his knowledge was based on memory going back to childhood.

'I used to watch your great-grandmother do this at the old stone sink in the kitchen. She was luckier than I am, smaller hands. The shop always leaves these bits in.' He displayed the bits he had pulled out from beside the spine.

'What are they?'

'Ask Mrs Shaw.'

'I wonder what she's doing for Christmas.'

'I wonder.' His thoughts strayed, and he brought them back to the matter in hand, drying the bird with kitchen paper and arranging it for roasting.

'I hope she's having a lovely time. I might be in her form next year.' She paused to put Ziggy out into the living-room. 'You will get chicken later. But no bones.'

'He had a go at Bone this morning; I swear his toothmarks are in my ankle still.'

'They eat bones when they catch birds, wild cats do. Why not chicken bones for tame cats, Daddy?'

'Cooking makes them brittle and splintery.'

Charlotte, cutting into sprouts across their stems, said, 'You know about a lot of things, don't you?'

'It'd be shame to me if I didn't by my age. But I shan't forget that because my uncle smacked me for giving a chicken bone to the dog. Caught me a slap on my bare thigh that tingled for hours. And he snapped the bone and showed me how it splintered. I suppose that's the way to teach.'

'With a cane?'

'Definitely.'

Charlotte rubbed her head against his shoulder. 'It's funny about people.'

'M'm?'

'I mean Mrs Lambert. She could be strict but she always seemed to be really a kind person. I don't see how she could come to do what she did.'

'You can't ever tell what people will do when they're pushed. Perhaps everybody's got a point where they snap. Thank God most people don't come to it.'

'What sort of Christmas will she be having?'

Charlotte sounded upset at this thought. He said, 'They try to lay on a good dinner for them. She's not in prison, only on remand as yet.'

Charlotte, who had been looking at her new watch admiringly, from time to time, now suddenly noticed what it said. 'Oh, *Sinbad* will have begun.' She had seen it before, but had underlined it in the programmes in red. 'I've got to see the bit where the genie looks in at the temple door. Come on, Daddy.' She rushed to turn on the television. Ziggy, who had romped in when she opened the door, turned round and romped out again.

Detective-Superintendent Bone hung up his apron and followed.

ABOUT THE AUTHORS

Susannah Stacey is the pseudonym of a writing team. Jill Staynes and Margaret Storey met at St. Paul's Girls' School in England where they wrote bizarre serials. Jill Staynes went to Oxford and then into advertising; Margaret Storey went to Cambridge and then worked as a secretary in publicity. Both women eventually found themselves teaching, and now they devote all their time to writing. Storey is the author of fourteen children's books, and Jill Staynes is the author of one. They live in London.